It Was No Goodnight Kiss.

It was a full-blown, magnificent mating of their mouths. It was spectacular!

Fredricka's insides quivered. She was so stunningly aware that it was Colin kissing her. All her senses were tremblingly alert. Suddenly he pushed her away.

She was stunned. She said, "Colin?"

"You are a dangerous woman."

She realized Colin was fighting for control. It was a little awesome that she could set him on his ear that way. She was tempted to see if it would happen again. But she wasn't sure what sort of power that would unleash. She hadn't been in control of herself. It had been Colin who put her aside so firmly. What if he hadn't?

The thought boggled her . . . and beckoned to her. Just what was she toying with?

Did she want Colin?

Dear Reader:

So many of you asked for him, and now you've got him: Shiloh Butler, Mr. November. *Shiloh's Promise* by BJ James, is the long-awaited sequel to *Twice in a Lifetime*. Not only do many of your favorite characters reappear, but the enigmatic and compelling Shiloh now has his very own story—and his own woman!

And coming in December... *Wilderness Child* by Ann Major. This tie-in to her *Children of Destiny* series winds up 1989 in a very exciting way....

I've been telling you so much about the *Man of the Month* program that I want to mention some other exciting plans we have in store for you. Celeste Hamilton will be starting a trilogy in December with *The Diamond's Sparkle*. And the next few months will be bringing you Desires from such favorites as Katherine Granger, Linda Lael Miller and Dixie Browning....

So go wild with Desire—you'll be glad you did!

All the best,

Lucia Macro
Senior Editor

LASS SMALL
TAGGED

SILHOUETTE *Desire*

Published by Silhouette Books New York

America's Publisher of Contemporary Romance

SILHOUETTE BOOKS
300 East 42nd St., New York, N.Y. 10017

ISBN: 0-373-05534-X

First Silhouette Books printing November 1989

Printed in the U.S.A.

LASS SMALL

finds that living on this planet at this time is a fascinating experience. People are amazing. She thinks that to be a teller of tales of people, places and things is absolutely marvelous.

One

In the muted shades of grayed colors of west Texas, the house sprawled in an oasis of greenery. At the back of the house was a large room that had French doors on three sides, and the ceiling was supported by several pillars. The floor was of red clay tiles, so the room was often cleared and used for dancing. It was a marvelous gathering place.

Between gatherings, the floor was covered with scattered rugs, tall palms were set about, and there were cozily placed easy chairs. Tables were arranged to provide a different luncheon place, or for cards or cribbage and there were also several chair groupings for reading or visiting... or to be alone.

One April day, Fredricka Lambert's cozy niche was near a bookcase in one corner. She was not deliberately hiding, she was just unseen. Therefore, while she hadn't intended to eavesdrop, she did overhear her hosts discussing her.

Mrs. Stoppenheimer said, "This is the fourth time we've had Fredricka on the circuit. I really can't find anyone else who might be suitable. Ethel and Jaff should know that," Mrs. Stoppenheimer said of Fred's parents. "Fredricka has unsuccessfully met every *single* man in most of Texas by now!"

"I know," her husband replied gently.

"Out here, there just isn't that much choice. The men who are suitable are married, or they fly into town on weekends and do their own hunting."

"I know."

"She's a charming girl. Very pleasant and malleable. I believe that's the problem. She hasn't any grit. If she had any at *all*, she would have brought Sling to The Question long ago."

"I know," Mr. Stoppenheimer murmured sympathetically.

Guiltily, Mrs. Stoppenheimer fretted, "Even with a houseful of her own, Ethel married off both our girls to good men."

"I know."

"What on earth can you find for Fredricka to do? Since Cougar's firm does all your accounts, what business can you concoct to keep her busy? Here it is only April, but I have her working on next year's *Christmas* cards—"

"I know."

"I've hesitated to have her redo the recipe files. She just did that a year ago. I don't cook that much nowadays, and the file is really in good order."

"I know."

Mrs. Stoppenheimer exploded: "You know, you know! *You*'re not the one all this falls on. You just tell Jaff, 'Sure. Send her out.' But *I*'m the one who has to hunt up escorts and find things to keep her busy."

"I—"

Mrs. Stoppenheimer threatened direly, "If you say that one more time, I shall scream!"

"I...uh..."

Mrs. Stoppenheimer sighed with exasperation and said. "I know."

Mrs. Stoppenheimer must have then given her husband some sort of look, because Mr. Stoppenheimer chuckled before he asked, "What about that foreman over at Blane's?"

His disgruntled wife replied, "He's twenty whole years older than she."

"We're scraping the bottom of the barrel."

"I'm at my wit's end."

Their voices faded as they left the room and went on into the hall beyond.

Curled tightly in her chair, Fred held her breath until she was sure they were gone. Then she slowly uncurled in the big wing chair that was almost hidden by the long fingers of a very vigorous palm. She stood, moving carefully, peeking to be sure no one else was there.

She put her drawing pad and pencil on the table by the stuffed wall bookcase before cautiously peering outside to see if anyone was around. With no one in sight, she slid out one of the nearby French doors to step into the riot of tall, barely controlled growth that had made this house such marvelous fun for the children years ago, when the Lambert family had visited the Stoppenheimers.

Fred was no longer a child. She was a grown woman of medium height with a pale skin that never tanned. Like all her sisters, Fred had the Lambert blue eyes, but she was the only member of her family whose hair was strawberry blond.

Fred had avoided acknowledging the niggle of suspicion that she might still be "on the circuit." That her parents were sending her around to stay with friends, to be introduced to a different set of men, in hopes of marrying her off.

She had allowed herself to assume that her visiting with old friends was being done to help out. Obviously that wasn't the reason at all. She was still on the circuit.

Watching to be sure she wasn't observed, Fred went down to the spring and sat on a rock in that quiet place.

At thirty-three, one had to be surprised to realize one was still being treated as she had been at eighteen. Thirty-three was almost double eighteen, and nothing had changed.

She was a daughter. In spite of the fact that Fred had been a business major and had a master's degree in design, she was still a daughter.

She'd spent six years in the Peace Corps because she couldn't refuse when they'd twice asked her to stay another term. The only reason she wasn't still there was that her daddy had fetched her home.

Now her parents were trying to marry her off.

Fred had been in love with Sling Mueller since third grade. She was still waiting for him to realize he loved her and ask her to marry him. That hadn't been possible for a long time, but now all the facets of his complicated family obligations were solved, and he was free to marry.

For a year she and Sling had been "a couple" to everyone but Sling. In this whole past year, there had been no reason for him to hesitate.

But he hadn't asked her yet.

Fred knew that being on the circuit was no shame. Marrying away from one's home place had always helped to keep the genetic strains from becoming too concentrated. So, as a young woman, there was no embarrassment in traveling around. There were lots of parties and smiling men, and a young woman was breathless with the attention and excitement.

The social circuiting had always been expected for the children of those families that lived outside of cities and in isolated places. Even at twenty-four or five, when Fred had made the route the third time. But at thirty-three?

It was a jolt for Fred to finally realize her daddy's friends had been camouflaging the true purpose of her "helping out."

"Fred-dee?"

Mrs. Stoppenheimer was yelling in her hog-calling, questioning way. Now knowing why she was visiting there, Fred was reluctant to face her hostess at that minute, so she sat still and pretended not to hear. That was ridiculous, because when Mrs. Stoppenheimer hollered, she could be heard in the next county. For such a small, ladylike woman to possess such a strident voice was always startling. Mrs. Stoppenheimer took some pride in it.

Fred held her breath so that a woman who was the distance of two city blocks away, couldn't have heard her breathe. After calling about ten times, Mrs. Stoppenheimer finally gave up, and there was silence.

Fred listened to the birds, the horses in a distant pasture, a motor roaring over yonder and an occasional shout. But no one called for Fred now; therefore there was silence. She sat on the stone by the trickling spring and allowed her eyes to see the patterns of nature while her mind converted them into designs.

So it wasn't until just before dinner that evening when Fred was given her sister's letter. As usual, Roberta was efficient in her communications, saying she was going to marry Graham Rawlins in less than two weeks, and at home. Fred had to wind up her business and be there.

"Wind up her business"? What business? Next December's Christmas-card list. That was indeed urgent business.

Roberta would be the last of Fred's four sisters who had married in just six months' time. None of Fred's sisters had known any of their men anyway *near* as long as Fred had known Sling. Yet, here they were, all married or marrying and Sling still hadn't realized he loved Fred.

What did her sisters know that she didn't? How did a woman get a man to recognize that he loved her and wanted to spend his life with her, and, all this while, that life was frittering away?

That night at dinner, after the main course had been served, Fred ventured, "Roberta will be married in two weeks at home. Will it be all right if I go home then?"

"Why, yes," Mrs. Stoppenheimer replied. "Of course," she added. Then she said, "We will be going, too, you see. I tried to find you this afternoon to tell you about this and to give you Roberta's letter. I saw the D.C. postmark and her address, you know."

"But can we complete everything before then?"

"It all can just wait, my love. Roberta's wedding takes precedence over any of our little problems."

Mr. Stoppenheimer offered thoughtfully, "Graham is an Indian-er man. That makes him a Yankee. All those Lambert daughters have been marrying Yankees." He gave Fred a weighing look.

Mrs. Stoppenheimer's telling stare at her husband was censoring as she said soothingly, "Well, there aren't as many men down here since The War."

Fred knew Mrs. Stoppenheimer meant The War Between the States, which Yankees called the Civil War, but that was five generations ago and could hardly be blamed for Fred's not being able to find a husband this long afterward. But The War had always been a handy reason for resentment and excuse.

The night's dinner guest, who was already a reject, said, "Actually, Mrs. Stoppenheimer, there are almost as many Yankees down South now, as there are in the North." He gestured discreetly as he elaborated: "The transplanted manufacturing companies, the booming Southern towns and the service organizations that have been developed by ambitious Yankees who know a good thing when they hear it. And then there are all the retirees who are looking for the sun. It's been a marvel. It's getting so that the Southern accent sounds peculiar."

Mrs. Stoppenheimer drew in a sharp breath, but she didn't send her guest from the table. He wasn't one of hers.

Mr. Stoppenheimer slid in tactfully, "Roberta's intended is the one that played the piano at Georgina's wedding, right?"

Fred nodded.

Mrs. Stoppenheimer then could say, "He *is* very talented,"—as if that excused his being a Yankee.

To make it easier for Graham and his not being a Texan, Fred explained, "He was raised on an Indiana farm not far from Fort Wayne." That at least allowed him to be credited as a man of the soil.

Mr. Stoppenheimer asked, "Where's Fort Wayne?"

Fred supplied: "In northeastern Indiana, near the Ohio border. Mad Anthony Wayne built a fort there for protection against the Indians, who weren't at all pleased to have settlers moving in on them."

Texans had done pretty much the same thing, so Mrs. Stoppenheimer ignored that part and questioned, "'Mad'?"

"Probably because the Indians tended to resist." Fred kept her gaze on her plate.

The guest asked, "Wasn't he the one who said 'My country, right or wrong'?"

No expert on quotations, Fred replied, "I believe so."

The guest then said jovially, "The quotation does provoke some interesting substitutions, like 'My wife, faithful or sinful.'"

Mrs. Stoppenheimer put her hand on her bosom and inquired, "Is *that* what happened?" The guest was a divorced man.

He sputtered, "No, no, no. I was just saying that like Mad Anthony saying..." And he stumbled on rather ineptly, but he blushed.

That caught Fred's attention and for the first time ever, she introduced a new subject: "I wonder if Roberta will choose for us to wear the ancestresses' gowns for the wedding like the others did? I find those old dresses so pretty."

Mrs. Stoppenheimer replied, "I do hope so."

And the guest was rescued.

Since the Stoppenheimers were, at times, sensitive people, and always kind and dear friends, they didn't mention anything about Fred's being the *only* Lambert daughter still not married.

The next morning, before Fred was out of bed, she heard a plane land. She got up and went to the window facing the landing strip to see if she could recognize the aircraft, but to her it looked about like any other small one.

She took a quick shower, dressed, and was at the top of the stairs when she heard his voice. Pig Kilgallon was there—not Sling.

It was then that Fred knew, in her subconscious, she had always been expecting Sling to come for her. At college, during her six-year Peace Corps stint, and over these month-long sessions with her daddy's friends, she had always been "listening" for Sling to come. Someone had. And again, it was only Pig.

Pig was Fred's older sister Tate's age: thirty-five. He was a loudmouthed, redheaded good old boy who knew everybody and ran his own place with great efficiency. He played the oboe at the barest whisper of an opportunity, and it was always a surprise that Pig could play so well. He was big, ham-handed, red-headed and freckled. Who would ever believe such a man could make such delicate music?

Since the visitor was Pig and not Sling, Fred didn't hurry down the stairs to him. She followed the halls as Pig's bellowing voice came closer and closer. She could have found him blindfolded, because his voice volume was very like the lower registers of a steam calliope.

Fred walked into the enormous kitchen filled with busy, noisy people working at a midmorning snack for the ranch hands and making breakfast for the family—that is, Mrs. Stoppenheimer and Fred. Everyone else had had breakfast long before.

Unless there were strangers for a meal, all those who lived on the Stoppenheimer place always ate in the kitchen. There was one long, beautiful cherry plank table down at the window end of the kitchen, just the other side of the pantries. The chairs were already filling up. Pig said, "G'morning, Fredricka."

With his words, everyone else greeted her, and she darted self-conscious smiles and head nods in reply.

She never really looked at Pig because she thought he didn't approve of her. He'd told her she had no business going off into the wilds of Africa for the Peace Corps, and he'd gotten very close to violence in his confrontation with Sling over it. Unperturbed, Sling had said, "It's her life."

Fred had figured Pig's opposition to Africa was prejudice, since he'd been so opposed to her leaving Texas; but then he'd come to see her in that place, which was at the other end of time.

She would never forget the village people's excitement and agitation when the little plane had managed to land there. She had volunteered to go out and see what was the matter, and there was Pig! She'd been so homesick, and who had shown up but Pig! She'd laughed and cried, and he'd bellowed at her cheerfully, quite terrifying the gentle villagers.

Pig had gotten along great with all those who had lived in that little hole-in-the-wall part of Africa, and the kids had adored him. Pig had said it was because he was so gloriously redheaded. He had pitched in cheerfully, concocting drying racks for the cloths, singing boisterously and mesmerizing them all with his oboe. And afterward, he'd helped Fred find markets for the villagers' fantastic weavings and fabric designs. He'd been a great help.

Now at the Stoppenheimers' place, and in microseconds of remembering that other time, Fred looked up at Pig and found him watching her critically. He told her, "You're too skinny."

She snorted. "Anyone your size would think a woman who is only ten pounds overweight is skinny."

In a soft voice he'd never used before, she heard him say, "Any woman who can distribute an extra ten pounds as nice as you ought to try to see what she can do with twenty pounds."

That made Fred blush. Hardly touching her, Pig had maneuvered her through the busy, talking, settling people so that she sat across from him. Every time Fred looked up, Pig was watching her, and her glance fled from his. His look was always so intense. It was as if he knew her soul.

One of the kitchen helpers brought her eggs and bacon—with French toast and maple syrup. All the hands complained: How come they hadn't gotten suchlike for their breakfasts? All they'd gotten was "burnt oatmeal."

That got the expected rise out of the kitchen staff, and there were lots of protests and countercomplaints and swearings about ribs that poked through their very skins, they were that underfed.

Since they were all lean, hardworking and well-toned, there were scoffings, with gigglings from the young women on the kitchen staff. That brought offers to take off shirts and prove the ravages of hunger. Which made Mrs. Stoppenheimer say, "Now, boys..."

That's how it went every meal. And as usual, the men teased Fred for sleeping so late. There it was, they pointed out, almost nine o'clock already, but *they*'d been up since dawn, working their fingers to the bone.

The men weren't in the kitchen very long, considering all the chatter they managed, but they cleaned off the platters of freshly made iced hot rolls, drank the steaming coffee and were gone. The kitchen staff began to clear away, leaving the Stoppenheimers, Fred and Pig still at one end of the long table.

Pig was saying, "So if you can spare Fred, I can take her back with me today. That'll give her a week before all her sisters descend on the home place."

The Stoppenheimers agreed, and as usual, Fred was never consulted. She was packed up and sent off to the plane with fond farewells and the expectation that she'd be back after the wedding "to finish up."

Because the Stoppenheimers were the way they were, they hadn't allowed her to pack all her things: "Now you're not going to need that till you get back." That made it clear that they expected Fred to return. They made it easy for her to do that. If she had something else to do, she could send for her things; but if she didn't, she had the excuse to return. That made Fred a little teary. They would go to such lengths to make her feel welcome at their place when they had not one idea of what on *earth* to do with her. But they loved her.

So as Pig lifted the plane into the sky, it was with fond eyes that Fred looked down on the toy house, so diminished by height and distance as they flew away.

With Pig, one never got to go directly home. He always had something to show her, as he had in Africa. There they'd gone out and around and about, looking everywhere it was safe for them to go, and it had been as if they were a film crew for *National Geographic*. Marvelous. Unreal. A real consciousness-raising time.

But now, flying across western Texas with Pig, Fred found he wasn't quite as loud and boisterous. He saw everything and pointed out the more interesting things on the April landscape. They flew low enough to watch the wide plains, and the stock and wildlife that moved at the sound of the plane, but Pig flew high enough not to startle or stampede the creatures.

There were wild horses. Fred thought what a sight it was to see wild horses running free. Then she thought they ran not just to have a reason to run, but because they'd been hunted by plane and were probably terrified of being shot by cattlemen who wanted the grazing cover left for their herds. This was confirmed when a mare hid her colt in a bush and then ran on to distract the plane from the colt.

Pig lifted the plane and banked around, handing Fred field glasses, and she watched as the mare circled back, got the colt and ran in another direction.

Texas wasn't too different from Africa, with the conflict for territory between man and diminishing numbers of free animals.

Eventually Pig landed the plane near Kerrville, where his little green car waited. Silently he drove her home. And after her parents had hugged Fred, they hugged Pig.

As Fred walked tiredly through the big Lambert house, she knew again that it was unique. The solarium and adjoining birdcage were both two stories tall, and the wraparound porches held swings and rockers and reed rugs. Inside, the blendings of colors and the treasured paintings were soothingly familiar, and the careful mixture of chosen furniture with the family heirlooms made the place special. It was home.

Fred had her parents to herself for over a week, and Pig was around. But although Sling had called and said, "So you're back," he was four days getting there. That depressed Fred. Wouldn't a man who loved a woman want to see her as soon as he could?

But he came in the front door that fourth night, and there he was, just like always: lean and dark and dangerous. No wonder women went wild over Sling. But although he didn't seem to realize it, even yet, he was Fred's. He smiled at her and leaned to kiss her mouth in a soft kiss.

A silent Pig watched.

They sat and talked with her parents and Pig, and finally Pig did leave. Then her parents went to bed, and Fred had Sling alone at last.

Sling grinned at her and said, "Let's go out on the swing, I'm an outdoor man. I can only be inside just so long, and I get fidgety."

So they sat on the swing, and Sling sprawled over more than his half of it, with Fred close by. He draped and arm over her shoulders and hugged her. "My God Almighty, you're prettier than ever. Nice to see you again. How was it out yonder? Do they still have that water sluice? I just about tore my bottom off on a nail that one year when I was about eighteen."

Just glad to be with him, she grinned as she told him, "It's now lined with a hard plastic and so slick that sliding on it's like being shot out of a cannon—really terrifying. I think they keep the hands with that sluice. They all love it. You should hear them!"

"You getting a lot done out there?"

"They're just really sweet, but I don't do much. I got visiting out of my system in Africa. This is the place I long to be." There. That was a good opening for him to say—

"I do understand." He nodded profoundly. "I went out to Kansas not long ago, looking at a bull there to see if I want to buy his sperm for my breeding herd. It's a different place, Kansas. I was glad to get back to Texas."

"You go to Kansas for a bull? Why?" If breeding was what he wanted to talk about, that could be a jumping-off place for talking about marriage.

But he gave a dissertation on strains and weaknesses and genetic variance, and while it was interesting, it wasn't at all what Fred wanted to talk about.

When Sling said good-night, he hugged her nicely and said, "It's great seeing you again, Fred. The whole entire area has been blank without you around." And he gave her a very sweet kiss. He smiled down at her and again said, "Good night." Then he left.

Sadly, she watched him go out to his pickup and drive off. And then she went pensively up to bed.

How could a man look that dangerous and be so safe? He was a late bloomer. His time would come. How long would it take?

Fred's sisters arrived with their new husbands: Georgina and Quint Finnig, and Hillary and Angus Behr came down in the Sawyer company plane from Chicago with Tate and Bill Sawyer, with Bill's daughter, Jenny, and Tate's son, Benjamin.

They all settled in. Twelve-year-old Jenny and four-year-old Benjamin had been there at Christmas and had rooms in the attic. They were familiar with the house and the grounds, so they were busy from the time they arrived, and Benjamin discovered baby chicks.

Then at almost the last minute, the wedding couple Roberta and Graham Rawlins arrived from D.C. The Lambert house was filled with voices and laughter, and Fred realized why the Stoppenheimers had their help come into the house for their meals: only voices can fill an empty home.

The five sisters had always come together as if they were never separated, but now Fred noticed a difference. The three in Chicago had shared more. But the five still shared their special closeness, fondness and interest. It was nice to be home.

Pig came to greet the arriving sisters, and his booming voice was easily heard. And there was his deep laugh. It was interesting to Fred that although it was loud, his laugh was nice to hear. He brought along some Kilgallon kin the ages of Jenny and Benjamin.

And Sling dropped by to say hello and that he'd be there for the wedding.

It was another pretty day for the wedding, and Sling did arrive in good time. He didn't complain about this being the third Lambert wedding in less than six months, but everyone else did.

Someone said, "Another Yankee." That got a good go-around.

And in the discussion on gifts, another said: "I just went ahead and got what I gave to the others."

One said, "I settled on cash."

But the heartless reply was: "What a coward's way! For shame."

The Stoppenheimers greeted Fred as if she, too, was one of their own, and they said comfortably that she could fly back to west Texas with them.

And one man said to another male guest, "I've never seen your ugly face so *much* in one year. Thank God there's only one more Lambert to marry off." Then he called to the father of the bride, "Good thing you give good parties, Jaff, or we'd all revolt, having to be together so much."

Another man chortled, "My good blue suit hasn't been out of the house so much in all its life!"

But a lady complained, "What am I going to do with three extra dresses? We don't go this many places each year, this dressed up."

Ethel Lambert promised, "We'll give more parties."

Which only caused the complainer to object, "How can I wear the same things next year? All the styles will be changed again."

Then an older lady scolded: "It would have been nice if you'd scheduled the weddings a little better. It seems a shame to waste all these parties in a lump this way. There's no *new* gossip."

Another put in, "Well, I did *hear*..."

Which caused a burst of interest.

And after that, as the wedding music began, the guests paused with less emotion than they'd felt at the Lamberts' first double wedding, which had taken place just last November. The practiced witnesses watched with less sentiment as the five sisters came down the stairs like a now familiar bouquet.

But the words of commitment were still as stirring. Fred saw couples who clasped hands and exchanged poignant looks, and one of the couples had been having a lot of problems. Would hearing the vows again help?

And what about Sling? This was the third time he'd seen a Lambert wedding; didn't it give him any feeling of urgency at all?

She looked at Sling, who was lounging in the door of the solarium and listening to the canaries who were competing with the violins played by the Smythe family. He wasn't at all touched by the emotional high of the wedding. Not at all.

When the time came, the new bridegroom wasn't allowed to leave the reception. They all told the bride she could just go ahead, and they'd send Graham along in a while. They needed him to play the piano. It was astonishing how many of the guests then produced instruments. They'd plotted to play.

Sling danced with Fred, in his slouched, slow way, with her squashed against him. But he didn't breathe fire from his passionate furnace. He talked. With her soft body squashed against his manly chest, he asked her, "How do the Stoppenheimers' cattle look?" He asked things like that. Fred wilted a little.

It was Pig who rescued Fred from the saw-armed, toe-mutilating Ed Arnold. And Pig took her outside to one of the porch swings, took off her sandal to in-

spect the damage and found a Band-Aid for one toe—
after he'd kissed it well. And he'd looked up at her and
smiled just a little as she laughed at his foolishness.

He sat beside her and told her, "Tell me your plans.
Have you thought of doing anything with your own
designs?"

"Well . . . sometimes."

"A good, positive attitude." He frowned at her.
"Why not send some things over to the mill at New
Braunfels?"

"Why . . . I hadn't thought of that."

"Why not do it?"

That made her look up at him as she remembered
how interested he'd been in the designs in Africa. The
second time he'd gone out there, he'd even brought a
marvelous variety of bold fabric paints along with
some solid-colored materials so that the people could
paint designs on the plain fabrics. The village people
had been amazed by the colors. Exuberant. And it had
been very festive and exciting as they'd worked with
Pig's gifts.

Fred would never forget the materials hanging in
long strips from contrived drying racks, and how they
had fluttered in the breezes like banners for an event.
With Pig there it had been one. He'd made it so, and
he'd played the oboe.

Pig had brought two lambs for them to raise and
breed for their wool, but in the language gap and the
festive feeling of seeing the cloths drying, the lambs
were killed for a feast. Although it had shocked Pig for
them to eat such expensively bred stock, he'd never
given one groan or grimace.

So there on her front porch, the rather tender, remembering smile Fred gave Pig touched inside him

and he said, "You're the prettiest of all the Lamberts."

"Phooey. If I was, Sling would dance only with me."

"Are you jealous?" Pig asked her seriously.

To Pig, she could admit it: "I feel that I am just like any other woman he dances with, that I'm not special to him."

"What do you care?"

"I feel insecure." She sighed the words.

"Tell him."

"He's always said my being so serene was such a pleasant thing. If I said his dancing with other women that way made me fretful, he'd be disappointed. I'd seem un-serene."

"*Un*-serene?" Pig questioned.

"Non?" She looked over at Pig, who watched her. She tilted her head and inquired, "Why haven't you ever married?"

"I've been waiting for the right woman to know I'm the only man for her."

"How will you know which woman?" she asked with interest.

"She'll tell me."

And Fred said a quiet "Oh," wondering whom he had in mind.

Two

The wedding guests finally allowed Graham to join Roberta so the pair could leave on their honeymoon. The witnesses followed the couple outside to pelt them with rose petals and some oblique jokes that even the older women understood. They watched the decorated car drive off, then stood around in the mild night, talking softly with quiet laughter.

Sling went for his Stetson, and Fred followed along, conscious that Hillary had tugged Angus away so that Fred could be alone with Sling. To Sling, Fred inquired, "Must you leave?"

"You know I have to get up early. I've stayed too late as it is. Your folks give good weddings."

Fred held her breath, but Sling went on. "It's nice to have the folks around from all over the state. I really enjoy it. It'll be nice at Homecoming too, with everybody back again. You coming back then?"

"I suppose." She stood, looking up at his face, knowing she was being a little pathetic.

Sling smiled down at her and leaned to kiss her lips, then he patted her shoulder and said, "You're a sweet girl, Fred." He put on his Stetson and ambled right on out of the house, leaving her standing where he'd left her.

She was about to go up to her lonely room and sit leaning on her window and be unhappy, but all those people who'd complained about having to attend still *another* Lambert wedding came trailing, talking, back into the house. There they all settled down and stayed and stayed and stayed. It didn't seem they'd ever give up and go home. They became very mellow and indulged in long reminiscing.

They'd all known each other forever, as their ancestors had on back into the years, so they knew each other very thoroughly.

It was always interesting for Fred to listen to them as they retold tales of the families and their tribulations. Jaff claimed that the stories changed. The villains got more villainous and the heros were becoming bigger than life. Ethel said it was all true, that that was how legends were made. Things were trimmed and "neated up" and made better.

And Fred listened to Pig. He told marvelous current stories of brave foolishness and risks, but he was never the hero. As Fred listened, she wondered why he'd been there with those men. That he had been there showed the man he was, too; but he never mentioned how he had been involved. He made it appear he'd just been an observer, taking notes so that he could tell the stories. And she thought how interesting it was that he was modest. That loud-mouthed man.

He had a good laugh.

Her pregnant sister Tate excused herself, saying she had to be up early to fly back to Chicago. And Hillary, too, had to go to bed. Georgina leaned her head on Quint's shoulder and smiled sleepily, but Quint mostly just looked at his wife as if he couldn't believe she was real. Fred wondered, Why couldn't Sling look at her that way?

Ethel and Jaff had the staying power to outlast their guests, and it was apparent their sons-in-law came from equally enduring genes. The men were fascinated by the Texas stories of struggles with rustlers and horses and contrary oil wells and hard-nosed people.

Georgina's Quint never said a word—or so few that no one really noticed. Angus, Hillary's husband, contributed a foreign Yankee story or two that, since they were stories of seagoing men, were received with interest, there in the middle of Texas, while Tate's Bill only enjoyed the tellings.

Pig was the last to leave. Fred was brought to remember that he had *always* been the last to leave. He'd been so laggard when he was younger that Jaff had once offered a room to him, but Pig never got the hint that he'd overstayed his visits.

It was going on three, that morning after the wedding, before the last of them had one last snack and sipped the last of the coffee. Even then, they stood on the porch and talked about the wonderful Texas air and the soft Texas night.

Finally it was just the family—and Pig, naturally.

Jaff called to Fred, "Lock the door after Pig when he leaves." And Fred found she was alone with just Pig. She was so tired and discouraged that she could hardly move.

"You going back with the Stoppenheimers?" Pig watched her as he always did.

She shrugged. "I suppose so. They're going off up to Michigan to see some friends, then they'll be stopping by here next week, if I want to go back with them."

"Do you wanta go back out there?"

She replied honestly, "I think I'll do as you suggested and submit some of my designs to the mills here in Texas. I'll go through those I have and see if any are good enough to send out, that way."

"I'll help you."

Fred knew that Pig could have a good counter opinion to her own, on which of her designs she should submit. She said, "I would appreciate your advice."

He accepted that rather formally with a single nod, then he told her: "I'll come by in the morning?" He questioned with a statement as Texans were prone to do. Such questioning statements were meant to confirm that the listener agreed or understood.

"Ten would be just fine. We'll be up early getting the Chicago people off. I just wonder if Benjamin is going to be able to let go of that baby chick?"

"Bet he takes it along."

"I doubt penthouse apartments on the shore of Lake Michigan are good barnyards. Tate would be the only one with enough backbone to make him leave it here. The rest of us are still too boggled over his being back with us again." Tate's ex-husband had stolen their son and kept him for two years.

"I was sure glad when Quint found Benjamin. That Quint could find anything." Pig clicked his tongue once to indicate how impressed he was with Georgina's husband.

And suddenly Fred *knew* that Pig had instigated his own search for Benjamin. She would swear that he had. It was exactly what he'd do for a Lambert in distress. He would deny it. How could she ever know for sure? And she put her hand on his arm because she was so touched by him.

Pig was almost paralyzed by her touch. His hand flew to instantly cover hers and he felt his blood rush to his core. She affected him that way. He swallowed and tried to breathe quietly. If he left her hand on his arm, he would begin to shiver, so he lifted her hand to his mouth and kissed it. "G'night, Fredricka. See you at ten." And he hurried off before he was tempted to carry her away with him.

Fred wandered around, turned off lights, then climbed the stairs to her room and stood at the window for a while. She was where she had thought she'd be, hours ago, after Sling had left in such a nastily friendly way. She had planned to come up there then and stand just this way, to mourn out the window at the night. So here she was, finally, but she wasn't quite as zonked as she'd expected to be.

In fact, she was nicely tired and rather looking forward to Pig going over her designs with her the next morning—*that* morning. It was almost four o'clock!

She stripped bare, smoothed cleanser over her face and scrubbed if off with a terry cloth. She crawled into bed naked, stretched her tired muscles and slept almost instantly.

Benjamin wakened her. He climbed up on her bed and sat next to her chest to tell her, "Mommy said I may *not* take my Chicken Little home with us."

He was looking for backup, Fred recognized that. One owed one's sisters loyalty, so Fred thrust aside the temptation to be Benjamin's favorite aunt and said carefully, "Chicken Little might miss his mommy if you took him clear to Chicago." And as Benjamin began to desert her bed and leave her flat, Fred added, "He'll still be here when you come down for Homecoming just next month."

"We're coming back?" He looked back at his ordinary aunt—not his favorite, but still kin.

"For Homecoming."

"And Chicken Little will wait for me?"

"He may grow a little. I'll send you pictures."

"But I can't take him with me?"

Cowardly Fred didn't reply; she just shook her head a very tiny bit.

Benjamin gave her a penetrating look, then left the bed and managed to reach up and turn the knob on the door, open it and slip through, closing it precisely. Fred wondered whom he'd accost next.

Jenny tapped next and came to Fred. "Has Benjamin been in yet?" She was full of laughter, this darling twelve-year-old child of Bill's.

Fred narrowed her eyes at Jenny. "If you're here for a chicken, forget it."

Jenny laughed out loud.

After breakfast Tate took Benjamin out to the chicken yard and told Benjamin to say goodbye to

Chicken Little. He picked up one of the chicks and cuddled it mournfully. Fred watched. She knew that Tate had a reason for doing this. Then Tate took the chicken and pretended to put it down, but cupped her hands and said to Benjamin, "Now which one is Chicken Little?" He looked at the puffs and picked up one and beamed.

But Tate opened her hands and showed him the other one. He laughed as he put the second one down and reached for the first one. Then Tate said, "He ought to be here with his family."

Benjamin understood, because during the two years his father had had him, he'd missed Tate. He'd never forgotten her. So now he nodded and agreed. Then he kissed all the chicks and was willing to leave.

But at breakfast Jaff said, "Pig was here earlier and left these." He gave Benjamin a fluffy little chick, a toy with real feathers. It was so perfect that Benjamin laughed out loud as he said, "Mommy, can I take *this* one home?" And his eyes danced with mischief, since he'd "won" the debate.

Tate laughed with him, appreciating Pig's tact.

Then Jaff said, "Jenny, Pig said this was for you so's you'll remember you're now part Texan." And he gave her a lapel pin with blue stones and green enamel that represented a bluebonnet.

There were exclamations: "That Pig!" and "How clever!" and "Where on this *earth* could he have found those things?" and "He is just so sweet."

Fred was sorry it hadn't been Sling who'd made such a good impression on her family. But she smiled that Pig was so thoughtful.

The whole Lambert family went out to the airport where Bill's plane waited, ready. As those leaving climbed aboard, those being left behind called, "Hurry back!" and the Chicago-bound ones yelled, "We'll be here next month for Homecoming!"

The parents and Fred watched the plane taxi off to the runway and take off to become a speck.

Ethel said, "I wish they'd split up and take two flights."

And Jaff said, "They'll be fine."

Ethel put her arm around Fred and said, "I was never easy those six years you were so far away."

"Be careful, Momma, I'm your old-maid daughter and I'll be underfoot forever."

Jaff hugged them both and said, "Good."

When they got back home, there was Pig on the front porch, sitting on a swing and looking like he was a permanent fixture. He got up and welcomed them as if it was his house.

Fred laughed. "Pig's here."

"Yes." Her daddy slapped Pig's shoulder in affection, and her momma hugged the big man. He looked at Fred in a waiting way.

She was awkward because she was vividly remembering what a fool she'd made of herself in Africa when he'd first flown in. He hadn't notified her that he was coming, and no one had any idea who would be in that plane. Fred had gone out to see why anyone would stop off there, and it had been Pig. She had laughed and cried and had been really silly when she had seen who had come to that place where she'd been so alone.

Now he was on her front porch and watching her expectantly. What did he expect of her? He said, "G'morning, Fredricka." His voice was kind.

Why couldn't she just say hello and be easy with him? Well, she knew why. It was because of that time he'd kissed her over ten years ago. That was why. She blurted, "Have you had breakfast?"

Pig nodded. "Such a long time ago, my stomach has forgotten what food means." Then he bit his tongue because it betrayed the fact that he'd had little sleep, getting only the vital things done so that he could have the time today to be with Fred.

But no one noticed that or asked him why. They all went into Rosita's pristine kitchen, where she greeted Pig with a hug as if he was family. She made no objection to fixing him a midmorning breakfast. Nobody ever asked Ethel to cook anything because she botched things so awfully.

Pig ate with relish, while the others talked about the wedding. They marked who wasn't there and why, and who was there and how they'd looked. And Jaff complained about the scant gossip supplied by the group, who'd seen too much of each other to be able to offer anything new.

After they left the kitchen, Pig waited downstairs while Fred fetched her sheaf of designs from her room. The house help were stripping beds and cleaning, so Fred laid out her designs in the only room available—the solarium. She propped designs against things and laid them on the floor with narrow passages for feet. She had already chosen the ones she wanted to submit, and she was impatiently curious about which ones Pig would select.

He took his own sweet time. So he was there for lunch. Rosita said, "It's a good thing you're here, or I wouldn't bother feeding these bird appetites."

Pig smiled. "You're the only reason I come to the Lamberts'."

Rosita burst out laughing and so did everyone else, with Pig grinning widely and just waiting.

But Fred hadn't recognized the joke. "What's so funny?"

Rosita said, "He comes here for the food."

Fred didn't see the humor in that. Not enough to make her parents and Rosita laugh so. Puzzled, she protested, "He does! Everybody does. Daddy had to give you their firstborn in order to keep you from taking any of the scandalous bribes people have offered you." She frowned as she accused, "You are so unscrupulous and disloyal *that you listened to them.*" Then she sighed and smiled a little. "But you sure can cook."

Rosita was bubbling laughter, but she only replied, "I know."

With Pig there, the lunch was easy and the exchange of conversation light.

That made Fred think of Sling. Why couldn't he be there instead of just Pig? Sling would sit there, shoveling Rosita's genius food into his mouth—and he wouldn't say one word. Actually, for company, Pig was better. Fred looked at him. Pig was a nice man. "Where on earth did you get those gifts for Benjamin and Jenny?"

"As soon as Benjamin saw those chicks, I knew we had trouble. So I had plenty of time. And I couldn't get the chick for Benjamin without getting something for Jenny. Girls that age like something different, and the bluebonnet pin seemed to fill the bill."

Jaff said, "You did a good job."

Ethel smiled at Pig and said, "You are brilliant, you know."

Pig grinned at her and replied, "That makes two of us who know I'm brilliant. We need to spread the word."

Ethel said, "I'm working on it."

Jaff laughed a smooth, amused chuckle that seemed to have other meanings.

So Fred inquired rather elaborately, "Do you guys have some private joke?"

Rosita supplied, "You played Jane too long."

Fred squinched up her face and tried to figure it out. "I'm supposed to quit standing around and take action?"

Rosita gasped in surprise: "She has a brain!"

Fred stared. "That's supposed to make sense to me?"

Rosita looked at the ceiling, then went back to arranging a fantastic dessert of strawberry trifle, which she served to the four, explaining, "I can't eat this today."

Suspiciously, Fred asked, "Why not? It's poisoned?"

Rosita told Fred's parents, "She might be struggling with reality. These could be the beginnings of resolution. Questioning is the first sign."

Fred frowned, for it was obvious that something was going on that she was supposed to know about, that her family understood quite clearly and were surprised she didn't. What? She had no idea. Their conversation went on around her while she sorted through all the happenings and all the people who'd been around, but she knew of nothing germane to her own self—not one thing that would involve her except for the designs that Pig would help her sort through.

She said to Pig, "Don't eat a second helping of dessert, we have to see about the designs."

He replied as if he were a tame man. "Yes ma'am."

Tame? Where had she found such a word to apply to Pig? For the first time in her adult life Fred considered the fact that Pig was not a tame man. So he was untamed. Unpredictable. Pig? She looked at Pig and she knew then that he wasn't tamed. How astonishing. Pig? But it was true.

The idea unsettled Fred a little. Was this why she was uncomfortable around Pig? A basic fear that he might scoop her up and carry her off? Pig? He never would. Would he?

He was saying: "—all right if I take Fred? It's been a while since she's seen one, and I thought she might like the chance."

"What chance?" she blurted.

They all looked at her, and her daddy asked with real curiosity, "Where you been, punkin? He's been talking about the rodeo over in Bandera."

"I'd *love* to go! Pauline lives over thataway! I haven't seen her in an *age*! That would be terrific!"

Pig was watching her with a rather elaborate expression of amazement and he confided to Jaff, "I should have dusted off a rodeo sooner."

Solemnly Jaff nodded while Ethel and Rosita laughed.

Fred squinted. It was another communication between them that passed right over her head. "Is Sling riding in this rodeo?"

Pig said rather shortly, "No."

"Daddy, you're not riding in this one, are you?"

"The horses and mules are rabbits. No thrill at all."

She pushed it: "Are you all plotting something weird? What's going on?"

They all acted startled. Fred studied them. Were they a little too startled? Were they up to something? She sighed. It was like Christmas gifts—she'd just have to wait it out and then be pleased. She'd better start practicing delighted surprise when she scrubbed her teeth.

Fred and Pig argued for two days over which designs she should submit. And she remembered one she'd left at the Stoppenheimers'. So Pig flew her out there so that she could gather the rest of her things, for she knew she wouldn't go back for a while.

When they got back home, Sling was there. He greeted Pig with "While you were out running around all over Texas, that stock went up four points before it dropped, and you missed it. You lost about six thousand."

Pig replied, "No problem."

Sling asked, "You can let something like that go?"

"Like I said, it's no problem. What're you up to?"

"I made enough to clear up my last debt, with a little left over. From here on out, it's free sailing."

Fred was so happy, she got teary. Now Sling could marry her. She sat and grinned and wished Pig would go home. She tried to think of any leverage she might have to bargain with her guardian angel, so that Pig would leave.

Sling got up. "Long day. Good to see you all. Good luck with the designs, Fred." He laid an affectionate hand on her head as he put on his Stetson and went cheerfully off the porch to his pickup and left—whistling.

Fred sat frozen. She was astounded. She went over her wish to her guardian and knew full well that she'd been perfectly clear. What had happened? Sling had come over there to tell her that he was debt free! And she had arrived with... Pig. Did Sling think she was interested in *Pig*?

But Sling hadn't been sad. He'd been whistling.

Pig didn't stay long. Supper was quiet. Fred went to bed early and lay wakeful. Sling was debt free. He might want to fix things up a little at his place, but he would be coming around soon and telling her that he loved her. They would marry soon and she'd be Fredricka Mueller.

Pig came the next day, and he was quiet and watchful. They packaged up the designs, and Pig took her into town to the post office. They left the post office and stopped to grin at each other and shake hands.

It was that weekend that Pig took her to Bandera to the rodeo. It was really a gathering of people in the area just for fun. And the pair had a great time. They saw all sorts of people they'd not seen in an age, and Fred had arranged to meet Pauline.

Pauline wasn't terribly interested in remembering olden times with Fredricka. She was divorced and quite obviously interested in Pig. Fred knew her annoyance wasn't jealousy; it was just that she looked forward to a nice, friendly chat with her old friend, and here was Pauline hanging on every word Pig said. It was ridiculous.

Fred knew that what she ought to do would be to go over and ride in the chicken scoop. Instead of a real chicken there were beanbags with feathers. The ladies had objected to using real chickens. Fred had never tried to scoop up a chicken from horseback, and she hadn't been on a horse, really, in over eight years. But trying would be more interesting than sitting, listening to Pauline trying to entice Pig.

She got up, and Pig's big hand had her wrist before she could blink. He said in a strange, soft voice that carried under the noise, "Where're you going?"

"I'm going to ride in the chicken scoop."

Pig didn't say "Oh" and let go. He said to Pauline, "Fred's restless and I have to monitor her for her daddy."

That made Fred *furious*, because he'd made her sound like an intemperate twelve-year-old. She stood tall and killed Pig with a glance. He smiled.

In one corner of her brain, which was a busybody and kept track of silly things, she thought that Pig Kilgallon *really* wasn't tamed. He'd fooled everyone. Everybody had thought he was very like a large family dog. But it wasn't true.

He took Fred's arm in a no-nonsense grip and walked amicably alongside her, as if they were friends, and he said in that soft voice, "You're not riding in any chicken scoop. Forget it."

She breathed heavily a time or two, then subsided and obeyed. Damn. She should have just gone on and tried it. Tate would have. But Pig would have caused a scene. He wouldn't let her. He was bigger.

He shook her arm minutely for her attention. "For being a good girl, I'll buy you a Popsicle. They have green ones."

How had he remembered the only vice she possessed? But just in time, she remembered she wasn't a child to be rewarded like one, and she told him "No thanks. I'll have a beer."

She hated beer. They both knew that. But he bought her one with such a benign smile that she drank the nasty stuff.

Pig watched her with such inner delight. She did drink it, and she got just a little tipsy—on one beer. He was absolutely charmed by her. By the time she got it all down, it was too late for the chicken scoop, so she asked for ten dollars and sang with the band. Anyone who gave the band ten dollars could sing with them— with the mike turned down—and there was a line of ten-dollar holders waiting.

She chose "The Eyes of Texas" and, since that was the unofficial state song, she got a rousing, standing ovation. Lamberts were smart. They knew how to tilt odds.

She had another beer, confiding, "It's easier after the first one."

At two in the morning, he carried her into the house as she was singing "Red Wing" and crying. Her parents met them on the stairs and Pig explained, "Escaping from a cocoon can be traumatic."

One hand waved her boots at her parents, and Pig took her into her room. Her parents followed. Pig's humor almost spilled from his eyes. And her parents patted him and shook their heads. He whispered, "She'll probably have a hangover. She had two and a half beers."

That set the Lamberts off into a wave of smothered hilarity that almost wakened Fred, who was fast asleep in her clothes.

* * *

Fred awoke the next morning, quite surprised she was in bed in last night's clothing. She felt great! She got up, stripped, showered, dressed and tripped downstairs. Rosita and her parents viewed her with tolerance.

"Good morning, I'm starved. What time did I get home, and how?"

"You don't remember?"

"Of course I do. Pig brought me home and carried me up the stairs and pitched me on my bed. I was exhausted! Did you know the second beer isn't bad? What did Pig mean about me getting out of a cocoon?"

They shrugged. They also made church by the skin of their teeth. Fred took the opportunity to tell her guardian angel that she had asked that Pig leave that one day and the guardian had left Pig there and sent Sling away, and what was her guardian up to, to be that confused?

Into Fred's mind came the word: *beer*.

Fred frowned, trying to decide if her guardian angel had been trying beer? Or if her own mind had been muddled by the dregs of it.

On Monday she received a phone call from Dan Surtes at the mill in New Braunfels. They'd gotten the designs and just wondered if she could come over to talk about them?

Fred said she'd be very glad to do that.

So on Wednesday, she drove over to New Braunfels. Dan was such an attractive man that Fred was a little sad she was already committed to Sling. She was formal with Dan and very businesslike, and he made it clear that he could be interested. They had lunch, and she met people who were very involved in business functions. They were sharp and clear, and their obvious aptitude made Fred feel a little sluggish.

Dan asked Fred, "So you were in Africa six years. What did you learn there?"

She replied, "That people are the same everywhere. That people are clever and that they're survivors. And the villagers are still my friends." And she thought: what a feeble reply.

But it was what Dan wanted. "Your designs show a strength that is exciting to us. We want them. But we have other applicants. There'll have to be a decision by the end of the month. Will that be all right?"

She forced herself to ask, "How many designers are in the competition?"

Dan was open about it. "We'll select several. We have designers on the staff now, of course, but we always look for new and exciting designs that are different. You're a surprise to us. We thought you might be a man, your designs are so bold. Is there an African influence?"

She shook her head. "These designs are from before I went to Africa. I really did very little of my own work while I was there. I didn't want to influence their designs. I was interested in getting theirs done and marketed."

Dan asked curiously, "How did they do?"

"Extremely well," she replied. "Several of the villagers have learned to speak English quite well, and they are the ones to represent their village in the markets. That was our goal. In this, we were very successful, but the villagers wanted it and worked very hard.

I was lucky to have been a part of their great adventure.''

"See? That's what's in your designs: adventure.''

And Fred was thrilled. Tate would be proud of her.

Three

The May Homecoming drew an astonishing number of people back to that area not far from Kerrville. It was an isolated place—hill country, sparsely populated. The last two generations of kids had all gone to consolidated schools, riding buses through the countryside. Country. They'd all worked their tails off getting away from there to cities, and now, filled with a longing nostalgia, all those displaced Texans plotted how to move back.

At the Lambert house, Fred watched as her four sisters came home. The newlyweds Roberta and Graham arrived from D.C. and the three from Chicago—Tate, Georgina and Hillary—with their Yankee husbands and a couple of kids. There was laughter in the house . . . the soft feminine voices with the new sound of deeper, masculine tones. The whole family was home again.

It was again brought to Fred's attention how different she was from any of the others. Tate and Roberta were dark-haired, Georgina and Hillary were blondes, but she was a strawberry blonde with the white skin that was such a nuisance.

It wasn't just physical difference. Each of the others was a part of a whole: Fred was the oddball. Why her? Why couldn't she fit in and be like everyone else? Why couldn't she be secure and confident the way her sisters all were?

Fred looked around the house and knew again how special it was. All her sisters loved the house, too, but they were contented with only visiting there. With Fred it was different. She clung to the thought of the house. During those six years in Africa, the house had been a beacon. It represented security to her. Safety. It was home.

As they'd grown up, none of her sisters had planned to marry. Tate's first marriage had surprised even her. All of the Lambert daughters had planned for and been contented in careers, except for Fred. She had always longed to have a home and children. How ironic that she should be the only one not married.

All of her sisters had gone to their old rooms with their husbands, and Fred heard the murmurs of their different voices. She could no longer go and tap on a sister's door without intruding into another unit. Separate. Thirty-three and still alone, Fred felt as if she were rattling around in her too-quiet room.

She went to her window to stare out. The view was so familiar that she didn't need to look at it. When Sling realized that he loved her, would she magically become a part of him? Would she then be of a unit, separate like her sisters? Or would she still be this solitary?

That Thursday night, there was the usual comfortable Lambert open house so that all the neighbors and friends could drop by and say hello. Nobody but the Lamberts could put on such an elaborate bash and make it appear so easy.

Pig was the first to come along, glad to see them all. Redheaded Pig. He'd had a pet pig he'd carried everywhere when he was little and he'd really loved that creature. It was then that everyone had begun to call him Pig.

He'd brought his oboe along on this Thursday night, and it was Pig who coaxed Roberta's husband: "Come and play for us."

Graham's playing was near perfect. Everyone said so. But Graham shook his head and replied, "It's this piano," as he touched the instrument's keys with respect, and he sat down to play.

Fred looked around the Homecoming crowd as more instruments appeared. She was amused. It was a good bunch of people. All of those friends were as easy together as family, maybe easier. Sling wasn't there. Fred sought her mother. "Sling was invited tonight, wasn't he?"

Ethel's gaze rested on her precious daughter. "Yes. Perhaps you should call him." And Ethel dreaded that. How could Sling have done this to Fred?

Fred did call Sling, but the phone just rang and rang.

When she had gone away to Africa, she'd thought maybe that would make Sling miss her, make him realize she was competent and could be independent of her family.

When she had come home, Sling had said, "Nice to have you around again." He'd said, "What're your plans?" But he hadn't said anything about loving her. Or about marrying her. Or about any plans of his own that might include her.

Frowning a little with her remembering, Fred looked up just as Sling came in the front door, removing his Stetson. He was something to see, that slow-moving, long and lean man. A breathlessness hampered her lungs. Why was he so obtuse? Well, he would be with her this whole weekend of Homecoming. There was something planned for every single minute, and Sling would escort her.

Sling smiled at everyone who greeted him, but he didn't glad-hand anyone or slap their shoulders. That was what Pig did. And as if conjured by Fred's thoughts, Pig was suddenly by her side. She gave Pig a quick, rather absentminded glance as she started toward the door—and Sling—but Pig put his hand on her arm and said, "Let him come to you."

Pig's words caught her attention because his voice was soft. That was the second time Fred ever remembered him speaking in that way. Pig never spoke softly. He was a shouter. She gave him another blank stare, and he winked at her. It was a quick, sober, do-it kind of wink.

Why was it that everyone thought they could tell her what to do? She again started for the door, but Pig's big hand went around her arm and he held her there, by him.

To Fred's knowledge, Pig had only once before touched her in that way, and that was in Bandera when he stopped her from entering the chicken scoop. He'd never shown any sign of male dominance over her. But there had been that one time, at a back-to-college dance before her senior year, when Pig had worn Sling's jacket and hat in the dark just outside the gym, and he'd kissed her. His kiss had about blown off the top of her head, before she realized it wasn't Sling—it was *Pig*!

That had been over ten years ago, and still, she vividly remembered her astonishment. Now, rather than make a fuss, Fred subsided and waited. She fumed a little inside, but she did know it really would have been unladylike to have plowed through all those people to get to Sling, and she would have looked so...obvious.

It seemed to Fred that Sling greeted every single other person in that place before he got around to even seeing that *she* was there, in the Lambert house, and then he said first to Pig, "All set?" By that time, the smile on Fred's face was getting tired. But Sling, that gorgeous man, finally looked at her and said, "So here you are," just as if he'd been searching for her. But she'd heard him greet how many others just that way.

She tilted her mouth up, and he leaned his head down and gave her a nice little dry kiss and smiled at her. But he didn't put his arms around her and hug her against that hard body. He didn't say "Excuse us," to Pig and take her outside to kiss her improperly. Sling wasn't that kind of man.

And she *was* glad that he was restrained. She would be embarrassed if he courted her too obviously in front of all those people. He had kissed her just as he always had. He didn't go wild and try to seduce her with every kiss, like some macho man. In fact Sling had never kissed her the way Pig had done that one time, which had been so embarrassing.

Pig still had his hand wrapped hard around her arm, and she pried at his fingers as she asked Sling, "Are you hungry?"

After not seeing his woman for endless days, any other man would have taken up on that remark and said something intimate, but not Sling. He said, "I had a little supper but I could use some of your momma's cooking."

"Momma doesn't cook. You know Rosita does that. Momma only tastes."

"When her taste buds okay it, you know it'll be good."

Pig said, "Fred made the goulash."

Sling raised his eyebrows in disbelief and asked, "Your momma check it out okay?"

That offended Fred a little, but Pig had to go and say, "I did."

Sling laughed and kidded, "That's no recommendation. Pigs'll eat anything."

Then Sling turned away, so Fred knew he didn't hear Pig reply, "Not this Pig." Sling didn't hear, because Pig was still using that strangely quiet voice.

Fred would have trailed along after Sling as she always had, but Pig still had her arm in custody. She said, "Let go."

"He'll expect you to follow him, just like always. Fool him."

She protested, "I haven't seen him in days and days!"

"Then a couple more minutes won't make any difference."

Pig was right. Fred could be a little aloof. Be aloof? She'd been out of town—out of the *country*—how many times to make Sling really miss her? That hadn't worked especially well, so far. She started off again, but someone came along to ask her questions about herself, like how much she'd made on her job and why hadn't she gotten married this year, since all her sisters had.

Pig interrupted, and in his booming Pig voice, he took over the conversation and asked appallingly personal questions right back. He offended the questioner, who turned and wiggled away through the crowd in something of a huff.

Chidingly, Fred shook her head at Pig and asked in a very patiently reasonable voice, "How could you ask a mother of five children if she was pregnant again?"

He appeared surprised. "I was just making polite conversation."

"There are acceptable forms of beginning conversation—personal questions aren't the way. It's none of your business what her husband made last year."

Pig smiled.

Fred considered that those had been similar to the questions the woman had asked *her*, and she tried not to smile as she looked at Pig. He had a lot of freckles and his carroty hair would not lie in any order at all. While Sling had been cast in bronze by Someone who had known what He was doing, Pig had been put together by an amateur, as a trial form, in clay. He had never been smoothed out. He was big and hard and rough. And his fingerprints would be on her arm for days.

Pig went back to his oboe, and in the crowded house, the sisters met and visited together in pairs or bunches, catching up and commenting. The party went on. It was late before the crowd began to thin. The musical ones were the last to leave. So Pig and his oboe were still there, with the dregs of the crowd sitting around in the solarium, when Sling sprang his surprise on Fred. He said, "Guess who's coming to the Homecoming?"

"Who?" was Fred's logical response.

"Sheila Knowles."

Fred faltered. Sheila had been class Queen to Sling's King at high-school graduation. Fred was the only Lambert daughter who hadn't been Queen. Sheila was Queen that year. A tiny blonde, she was a doll. The contrast between her and the tall, devil-dark Sling had been exciting to just about everyone who saw them— but not to Fred. That had been the most miserable time in her life. Sling had had to escort Sheila everywhere, while Fred had had to make do with a series of dates that Sling had selected for her. It had been awful.

Sling was going on: "—so the committee decided we ought to do it like it was done before. I'll be her escort. Fred, I asked Pig to take care of you during this time. I knew you probably wouldn't have anyone lined up, since you've been away and out of it so long. I figured I'd help you out that way, since I won't be available."

To Fred, it was devastating. Sling still didn't realize he loved her. He was going to be with the newly divorced Sheila for an entire weekend—and Fred would be with Pig. Disaster. She couldn't get mad or cry in front of strangers. Or her family. Or Sling, who ought to be shot. Or Pig, who was strangely, excessively, quiet. Fred could only manage to reply, "I see."

Pig said, "I'd be honored."

Sling put his hands flat on his thighs and stood up as he said, "Well, that's settled. I have to go on over to San Antonio and meet her plane. I'll see you all to-morrow. Nite.'' He smiled at Fred, leaned over and kissed her cheek. "Nice to see you, Fred.'' He gave them all a big smile, and he left.

Her momma said, "Come help me clear off the table, Freddie.''

Her momma saying "Freddie'' almost triggered the damned tears that she hadn't allowed to spill. Ethel Lambert never remembered her daughters' names and called them all "precious'' instead. For her momma to not only remember her name but to use that fond corruption just showed that her momma *knew* what Sling's announcement was doing to Fred. Her momma was helping Fred to leave the room before she wailed and railed about Sling. Fred stood with dignity and followed her mother into the dining room, where nei-ther touched a thing but went on into the kitchen, past the crew working there, and out the back door to sit on the steps with the sleepily welcoming dogs and cats.

Fred said a shaky "Damn.''

Her mother said an agreeing word that Fred didn't know mothers knew.

They sat in silence for some time. Then the back screen door opened, and Pig backed out, carrying a tray of lemonade. "Rosita said to get this out of her kitchen *right now*, because it's in the way, and there's no place to store it, and it's too good a mix to pitch. So you gotta drink up. I added just a touch of gin.''

He sat with them next to Fred on the steps, and he played with the dogs, getting them all stirred up like he always did. One of the cats curled on his bumpy lap. It was a little cool with the Gulf breeze at night, and Pig's lap was probably toasty warm. Fred could feel his heat from over a foot away.

Gradually all the rest of the family wandered out into the cool May night and draped themselves on swings or rockers or steps. The moon was high and the night was silvered.

The pregnant Tate's husband was holding a sleeping Benjamin, and his daughter Jenny took up another one of the cats. Georgina's big, awesome, rather intimidating Quint went out into the yard and walked around, looking over the area; she followed him and they stood quietly talking. Hillary sat just behind Fred and leaned Fred back against her shins, and Angus sat beside them. Roberta and Graham were on one of the porch swings, and Jaff emerged from the back door to sit on one of the rockers.

Finally Rosita came out and ousted Jaff from her rocker, so he unwillingly moved to another. To Fred, it was the strange feeling of a gathered, supportive clan. No one said anything about Sling or Sheila or anything. They'd almost all traveled a long way that day, and the open house had lasted predictably late. But instead of seeking their beds, they were outside on the cool porch with Fred. It made her feel very loved. Pig was the only outsider there. As usual, he didn't realize he was intruding and ought to go on home.

With his customary lack of tact, and with both Jenny's parents right there, Pig said to Jenny, "Isn't it about time you were in bed?"

To Fred's surprise, Jenny said "Huh?" and looked at Pig. Then she smiled and said, "Oh. Yeah." And she excused herself nicely, wishing them all goodnight. As if by rote, Jenny's parents left then, with Bill carrying a completely lax Benjamin. Then Roberta said good-night and grinned at Graham, luring him away to her room. Quint was the one who rumbled

"Good night" as he took Georgina away. Hillary seemed reluctant to leave Fred, but Angus tugged her to her feet.

Rosita said her bed was lonely and she needed to comfort it. If it hadn't been for Pig, Fred would have had her parents all to herself, but Pig didn't appear to realize that. So Fred gave up. She started to stand, but her mother reached out and pulled her back down onto the step. Then *she* got up and said, "Come on, Jaff."

And since he was a wicked man, Jaff gloated, "Want me upstairs, do you?"

Her momma grinned at her daddy and said, "Oh, go ride a bronco."

Jaff almost replied, but only laughed a little. He said to Pig, "Nice to have you around."

Pig only nodded once in reply.

Her momma kissed Fred's cheek and her daddy ruffled her hair messily as they said good-night to her. It was the perfect setting to share with Sling. But he was on his way to San Antonio to meet Sheila's plane. Sheila, who had lusted after Sling all those years ago. Sheila, who was small and doll-like and adorable. That was where Sling was—meeting Sheila. And here Fred sat on the back porch in the silence. All were gone but her, the cats, the dogs, and the night with its moon. And the only man around was Pig.

She gave him a hard, disgruntled look. He was sitting next to her on the steps, his heat billowing across the space between them. She'd never been aware of any heat from Sling. She'd sat this close to Sling and not been scorched. It was rather vulgar for a man to be that hot.

He asked, "Are you going to stick around for a while after the Homecoming?"

It was really none of his business. She turned out a hand dismissively, acknowledging his comment but declining to reply.

He said, "Your daddy's had you out and running around all over the state this last year. Do you suppose he's been trying to keep you single?"

That was none of his business, either. She was silent.

"I have sometimes had the feeling that your daddy doesn't much care for Sling as a son-in-law."

That *really* wasn't any of his business! Fred started to get up.

But he put a hand on her shoulder and kept her there. "It's something for you to think on, Fred. Your daddy and momma haven't been red-hot about Sling all this time, or they'd have helped."

"You're an expert on parents?"

He had the gall to nod. "I've made a detailed study of my own, and you will have to admit parents *are* interesting people. I've come to the conclusion that parents have lots of things in common, and they... give...signals. You watch faces and gestures and listen, and they *can* clue you in. They might appear to give you a free hand, but there *are* those signals. You pay attention, now, and watch them around Sling."

"It's really none of your business."

"Well—" he chose his words with great care "—I don't want you to make any mistakes or marry the wrong man."

That surprised her. She kept forgetting that Pig was sensitive and cared about other people. It really touched her. And Sling trusted him. He'd asked Pig to take care of her this weekend. It was nice of Sling to see to it that she wasn't alone in all those couples. She said, "Are you sure you want to be bothered with me this weekend?"

"I'm more than willing."

He was still talking in that quiet way. He didn't seem like Pig. "Are you feeling well? You seem a little subdued."

"I'm learning not to overreact."

She'd never known Pig realized he was boisterous! That was rather hard to assimilate. He was trying to change. How astonishing! She wasn't sure a quiet Pig would be an improvement.

The dogs were exhausted by then, and went off to the barn to get away from Pig's excess energy. That was really what it was with such a man: excess energy. He needed ways to funnel it away from him. He was running his place mostly by computer. There was a time when he'd ridden horses or Jeeps all day, but now he was mostly at a desk. But that wasn't any reason for him to be quieter—he should be wilder. He'd always been rowdy, loud and busy. Now he lounged on the steps beside her with that cat on his furnace. He was really male.

He was old enough to be married, being thirty-five. "Don't you see anyone steadily?" she inquired. "It was an imposition for Sling to tie you down to me this weekend. You ought to be taking someone around who interests you. This isn't fair to you."

Pig assured Fred, "I'm not complaining."

"There's a limit to what one man should ask of another."

"I volunteered." Pig underlined the words.

"Sling didn't ask you?"

"No. I was at the meeting when it was decided that Sheila would need an escort."

"And poor little bitty Sheila can't hire a car and drive herself around here, where she grew up and where she knows everyone."

"Heavens to Betsy, no." His slow, strangely soft voice was shocked.

And Fred burst into tears. She could have just died. But Pig removed the cat from his lap and put Fred there. And he held her tightly and rubbed her back, and she wished to God he was Sling. Since Pig was Pig, she wasn't at all embarrassed. He, too, was a loser, and he'd know just how she felt.

But surprisingly, Pig knew all the right things to say in that particular circumstance. In that new low, soft voice, he told her she was a nuisance. That she was getting his shirt all wet and it was a clean one not worn before that very day. And he said that it was just a lucky thing he had this week's clean handkerchief in his pocket, but she was only to use one side.

That made her laugh, but he'd waited long enough, so that she had cried enough, and she was satisfied. She blew her nose, and her breath shivered and she laughed shakily.

Before she was ready to be moved, he stood up, set her on her feet, kissed her cheek and patted her fanny as he said, "Time for good girls to be in bed. How about mine?"

That was so ridiculous that she laughed again. And her thanks to him were throatily tender. Good old Pig.

He didn't go back through the house with her, but stuffed his hands into his jeans pockets and walked off around the house to his pickup. It was the last vehicle there. She trailed him, walking along the porch, automatically "seeing" him out, then she sat in the swing on the front porch as he drove away down their lane.

She took one of the porch pillows and put it behind her back on one end of the swing and lifted her feet up. The cats had followed along, being curious, and they were willing to relocate with her. They purred, giving her a feeling of company.

Was Pig right? Didn't her daddy approve of Sling? Was that why she'd been sent back on the circuit? Why did Pig think her parents were disapproving of Sling? Had her daddy said anything? No, he wouldn't. That wasn't his way. She mused sleepily on what sorts of gestures and expressions parents gave to children. Parents. How fortunate the Lambert daughters had been in theirs.

Her mother came out onto the porch. Fred was so touched. She started to move, but her mother pulled a rocker over. Then Ethel put a plush throw over Fred and the cats before she sat on the rocker, just being there.

Fred offered, "It's nice to have everyone home."

"It's good to have you here."

Then Fred asked, "Do you approve of Sling?"

"Why do you ask that?"

"I don't believe I've ever heard you give an opinion."

And Ethel said, "You've known him a long time."

"I've loved him since we were in the third grade."

"No one else ever caught your eye?"

Fred laughed a little. "Pig. It was Pig before that. He was so interesting. So *busy* all the time. He was always up to something. How he loved that pig."

"He's a good man."

Then Jaff opened the screen door and said, "Come to bed, you two night owls. I'm afraid you'll gossip out here all by yourselves and I won't hear it."

"I thought you were opposed to gossip," Fred nudged.

Her daddy agreed, "Only after I've heard it."

Her mother just sat, waiting to see what Fred wanted. So Fred got up, arranged the throw for the cats and then she smiled at her mother and father. "I was lucky I got you all."

"Likewise." Her dad just waited.

"Good night." She kissed them both and went on up the stairs to her room. It was a while before she heard them come up. When Fred was in bed and warm, she thought how nurturing they were. Then she remembered that her mother hadn't really replied to her query about Sling. Her mother had given a question as a reply, but she'd volunteered that Pig was a good man. Why hadn't her momma said that about Sling?

Fred puzzled over that, going over their conversation, and still puzzled, she went to sleep.

Just to show how absolutely off kilter Fred was, she dreamed erotically of *Pig*! Even just dreaming of him shocked her. It had to be the last lingering residue of that long-ago kiss that night by the gym.

Four

___

On Friday morning, and without Fred, the four sisters shooed Jenny and Benjamin out of the attic rooms and settled down to discuss a battle plan to help Fred with Sling.

Roberta opened the debate by saying, "Tate is really responsible. She intimidated Fred all those years ago and ruined her initiative. We have to use this weekend to teach Fred to be assertive."

"I'm responsible? How could I *possibly* be responsible for Fred being such an insecure namby-pamby? She's always been that way."

Georgina explained readily enough: "It all began during your Tarzan period. If you hadn't made Fred stand around for two years being Jane and screaming for help, she might not be such a wimp and she could handle this for herself."

"Well, I'll be darned! I thought Mother and Daddy had the *rest* of you all for *my* entertainment. How was I to know you were here for your own lives?"

The youngest, Hillary, looked at middle child, Georgina. "How like a spoiled first child."

"'Spoiled'?" Tate thoughtfully rolled the unusual word around on her tongue.

And Georgina commented back to Hillary, "How like a spoiled first child not to recognize criticism."

"Now, how could anyone find anything about me to make them critical?"

The other three looked at each other and shared disgusted noises. Being a lawyer and organized, Roberta questioned, "What do we do to help Fred?"

Hillary checked it out: "You each brought a killer dress?" They'd spent their lives swapping clothes.

Georgina promised, "Mine's surefire. She'll knock him off-center with it."

But the practical Roberta asked, "Are we sure Sling is the man for Fred?"

"No," Tate admitted, and the others gave agreeing murmurs.

Roberta pressed: "What if we shouldn't interfere?"

Tate shrugged. "A safe neighbor is what she's always wanted."

"Next to Quint, Sling is very nice looking. His body is great."

The recent brides all interjected: "Next to Graham." and "Next to Bill" and "Next to Angus."

So Georgina adjusted her statement: "Fifth down the slots, Sling is very attractive."

Newest bride Roberta put in, "There's more to marrying a man than his being attractive."

Hillary suggested, "It helps."

"Sling's debt free now, and solvent," Roberta mused. "That's important. Fred wants babies." Then she said, "Speaking of having babies, how you feeling, Tate?"

"More pregnant than last month."

And Hillary grinned. "I haven't told Mother and Daddy yet, but—"

They all whooped, so it was a while before they settled down and got back to discussing plots, none of which would work under *any* circumstances. They finally agreed they'd better just watch and then decide how to go on.

So they went downstairs and Fred asked, "Where were you? I looked everywhere."

And her sisters surrounded her.

It wasn't until afternoon that the sisters gathered in Fred's room to watch her try on their loaned dresses. All the colors were smashing with her strawberry-blond coloring. One was a pale green, another was black-purple, one a yellow-brown gold, and one the exact color of her skin. The cream one fit like a glove.

"Now, Tate, when did you ever wear this?" Fred asked in shock.

"Not lately," Tate replied as she patted her five-month bulge of a tummy.

Fred looked at herself in the mirror. The dress was lovingly clinging. It was a scandal—a decent scandal, but outrageous nonetheless. "You would never have worn this, and you know it. It's wrong for your coloring."

"What a detective you are!" Tate exclaimed passably. Then she admitted: "I saw it when I bought a wild, red dress for myself, and I knew one of you three light-haired ones would be able to use the cream.''

''So how come you gave it to Fred?'' Hillary inquired indignantly.

Tate smiled smugly. ''She's second oldest. Age has its privileges. Georgina has seconds, and you, Boy, have third choice.'' During Tate's Tarzan period, Hillary had been too young to be anything but Tarzan's found child, and on occasion Tate still called her Boy. It was a ludicrous label.

Sadly watching, Hillary commented, ''I don't believe Angus would allow me out of the house in that dress.''

''Let's ask him.'' Fred lifted the gown off over her head. ''Here Hillary, put it on.''

''I'm pregnant, and the prenatal influence of that dress might warp this child.''

''Pregnant?'' Fred's heart was in her eyes.

So the other sisters exclaimed, as if it were the first time they'd heard Hillary's news, and they all hugged Hillary. Tate complained that Hillary was horning in on her spotlight, just like always. When Hillary had been Boy, she'd been precious, too, distracting from the ''magnificent adventures'' of Tarzan.

Hillary explained, ''One does as one must in order to garner attention.''

Fred said, ''Both of you pregnant. It'll be nice for the cousins to be so close in age.''

The sisters smiled, but feeling Fred's envy, they didn't know how to reply.

Roberta brought them back to the business at hand. ''So. What about the dress?''

Fred said hesitantly, "I think we ought to have a male opinion. How about you, Georgina? Try it out on Quint."

"If I put on that dress, Quint might not let me stay here. If I wore it, Quint would believe I was bent on flirting with every man at whatever place we went. I don't dare."

Fred scoffed: "You allow men to dictate what you wear? And you all think I'm a coward?"

"Not a coward." Tate pushed up her lower lip in deep decision. "Just wishy-washy."

"What's the difference?" Fred flung out her hands indignantly.

"A shading," Roberta explained. "It's like honesty and integrity. A difference."

"I reject being wishy-washy. It sounds like a wimp."

Since that was exactly what her sisters thought, too, they were all quickly, busily examining and discussing the rest of the dresses.

Unwishy-washily, Fred declared, "I shall wear the *cream* to the big dance tomorrow!"

In the tone of voice that one used when asked if she knew the earth was round, Roberta remarked, "You'll probably cause a riot."

Fred smiled.

Tate suggested, "You could try the dress out on Pig."

Fred shook her head. "He wouldn't notice."

Roberta told her, "I believe he and Daddy've been out and about this morning. They'll be back soon. Why not try it out on them?"

"After all," Hillary mentioned, "Pig'll be escorting you."

"Oh, don't be silly. I'm not going to go anywhere with Pig. I'll just tag along with you guys."

"Not with Pig?" Georgina frowned.

"No."

With some drollness, Tate told Fred, "He bathes now."

Roberta was a little huffy. "He's always bathed!"

Tate calmed her. "We know."

Fred flung out her arms and asked the ceiling, "Who wants to go with a man named Pig?"

Hillary replied, "Most of the female population. Women are crazy about Pig. Didn't you know that?"

"Why?" Fred looked at the youngest sister with rather elaborate interest.

Hillary shrugged. "All I know is that women talk nice about Pig. When they see him they make sure he sees them smile at him. And they wait until he smiles back. They don't hurry past him but lag along, in case he wants to walk with them, or they see if he'll come and talk to them."

"They might talk with Pig, but they set their traps for Sling." Fred was sure.

"Well, he's single. To women, that's a waste."

"You're not trying to tell me women prefer Pig to Sling? There's a limit to what I'll believe, and that's not on my list."

Hillary said soberly, "I hear women talk friendly about Pig, but they don't talk about Sling. Why, I have no idea. They speak to him, but it's different. It's like they don't feel as comfortable with Sling as they do with Pig. I can't explain it any other way. They look at Sling, and they watch him, but they don't try for his attention like they do for Pig's."

It gave Fred something to think about. And in a very short time, she came to the conclusion that women knew Sling wasn't a flirt. He was unobtainable to most women. Sling didn't need women hanging on his arm. He was choosier than that Pig. Pig soaked up attention. He was so glad to have anybody talk to him at all that he was overly friendly. That was the difference.

They all separated to their rooms, and just as her other sisters were doing with their husbands, Georgina reported all their progress—the lack of it—to Quint. "There just aren't enough single men around who can compare to Sling. That's the *whole* problem. He doesn't have any competition. He can just sit back, and when he's ready, he can pick the woman he wants to marry. I just wish there was one decent man around to give him some competition."

"What about Pig?" Quint asked in his rumbly, carefully said words.

Georgina dismissed Pig as being no help at all. "Fred can't even 'see' Pig. She's known him all her life and he's more like a cousin than anything else. That Sling is stupid. He should have snatched up Fred long ago. I don't understand him at all. When he comes to his senses, how am I going to love him like a brother when I want to tear his hair out now?"

"I want you to love only me." Quint was serious.

Georgina gave him a slow, flirting look. "Why?"

So he had to explain, and since he wasn't a talkative man, he used his hungry body to make her understand. Georgina laughed in her throat the way that filled his senses with erotic excitement, and he made love to her in her old room at the Lambert homestead.

When she napped, Quint went down to Jaff's study, closed the door and sat down to go through a small, thin address book. Then, since Quint had committed his life to making Georgina's perfect, he made a couple of telephone calls.

But Quint wasn't the only man who was committed to a woman.

To begin the weekend festivities, there was a dance that Friday night, and it was held in the area meeting Hall, which was a rectangular, cement slab of a building and tin roofed. It was very utilitarian. And it sat on about the only unattractive piece of land in all of Texas. It was level and treeless. It took a long time to grow a tree in rock.

The Hall was maddening to any decorating committee who wanted to make a happening seem special. There just wasn't much that could be done about the building's relentless ugliness. Even feather palms seemed to give up and wilt a little when they were moved into that nothingness.

So besides the discouraged palms, there were always a lot of balloons and flowers. And the bands could be counted on to play loudly. Maybe that was why everyone always had such a good time. Everyone tried harder in order to compensate for the surroundings.

The Lamberts gave a dinner before the dance on Friday night. Fred chose to wear the pale green gown. It left no doubt she was female. The gazes of her brothers-in-law stayed on her face. Her daddy blinked. Pig cleared his throat and looked very sober. Her mother smiled, and her sisters told her she was gorgeous. Fred felt self-conscious.

Altogether there were about thirty people at the Lamberts' sit-down dinner. Two of the guests were Sling and, of course, Sheila. Sling was his usual self, but Sheila positively glowed, until her sweeping glance paused just past Fred, and quickly came back to that pale green dress. Then she managed to say in an aside to the second-oldest Lambert daughter, "Feeling a little competitive?"

But Fred made no reply or any response whatsoever. She was so furious that Sheila would make such an asinine comment that she didn't trust her tongue. But Bill had heard Sheila's remark. And so had Pig.

During dinner, Sheila was animated, darling, touchy-touch with Sling; and Fred relentlessly smiled the entire time. Pig sat next to her and was attentive. He ate one-handed and left-handed because he held Fred's hand the whole time. He never let go of that cold, clammy, nervous little hand.

Since Sheila hadn't been around for a long time, having lived clear up in Oregon for over six years, she was the center of conversation.

Fred thought bitterly, Sheila had *always* been the center of conversation. She radiated attraction. She drew stares. She sparkled. She made Fred nauseous.

"So. How's it feel to be back home again, Sheila?" some male voice asked.

Male voices were always asking Sheila inane questions in order to look at her and get her attention.

Sheila sparkled and said, "Just wonderful." And she turned all that voltage on Sling. "It's like old times." And she was skilled because she then refrained from underlining the whole situation by looking pointedly at Fred.

Fred quite clearly remembered that Sheila had been Queen to Sling's King. She didn't *need* to be reminded that Sheila was again being escorted by Sling, while Fred was with—Pig.

Natalie Comstock was Ethel's dearest friend and courtesy aunt to the Lambert daughters. She now looked coldly down the table to Sheila and inquired in a carrying, company voice: "With your momma up in Dallas now and your Aunt Bobby Lou in San Antone, where are you staying?"

Sheila sent a twinkling look at Sling, encouraging him to reply for her, but he was calmly eating and made no effort. So it was Sheila who said charmingly, "Well, you know how crowded everyone is. With all the kin back for Homecoming, there just wasn't any place, so Sling said I could stay with him."

There was a very empty silence. Then Natalie bent her most formidable matriarchal look on Sheila and declared in a no-nonsense voice: "That will never do. You will move into my spare room. See to it tonight, Sling. Do you hear me? How could you think to compromise Letty Pilgrim's daughter in that manner?"

Not only was Sheila startled, she wasn't at all pleased.

There was a disbelieving rustle, but no one ever crossed Natalie Comstock and lived. And although Sheila just about choked and did turn an unbecoming, mottled red, she said in a passable voice, "How nice of you." But it really wasn't sincere.

Pig's free hand rubbed his mouth hard and he shifted on his chair. Around the table there were several choking coughs, but nobody said anything. Then Ethel said, "You could have one of the attic rooms here, if you'd prefer." And she watched Sheila.

Fred's soul writhed, and her nails dug into Pig's right hand.

But Ethel knew what she was doing, for Sheila smiled fairly well and gently explained, "I've already accepted Mrs. Comstock's kind offer."

And Ethel gave Sheila a look that lasted just a mite too long before she said, "Yes."

Now there was no way, at all, that Sheila could wiggle out of staying with hawk-eyed Natalie Comstock. Sheila knew that. Here she was, thirty-four years old and a divorced woman, but Mrs. Comstock and Mrs. Lambert had very neatly locked her in. After that exchange, she couldn't decide whether to stay with a friend or anyone else, no matter how proper it would be, because if she did, she'd be rude to the Comstocks and the ricochet would go on to the Lamberts. In a thinly populated area, one minded one's p's and q's or she was ostracized.

Sheila paused—her cheeks had lost some of the infused color and even her temper had faded—as she wondered if she really wanted to come back to this area to live. She'd forgotten what it was like to be judged. The people around here were so close they were almost like kinfolk. They pitched in and helped, but they could be just as diligent in disapproval. So there was the anonymity of a large city and living unchallenged, or the closeness of an isolated area and having to mind their set rules of conduct.

Sling said nothing as he continued eating. His expression didn't change; it was no big upset. He nodded when he was told to move Sheila out of his house, and that was settled.

In that crowd of people, with the busyness of being served and plates being changed, the hum of conversation was cheerful and the soft laughter pleasing. Only Sheila and her archrival, Fredricka Lambert, were perturbed. The succulent food was wasted on them.

Pig asked if he could have the rest of Fred's steak, and she was glad to get rid of the thing. Then she had more room on her plate to push around the vegetables. To her, the only real people in that room were Sling and old whatshername. Fred felt as if she was only a shadowy image with no real substance; a pitiful wraith with no anchor—except, of course, Pig's big right hand, which wouldn't let go of her left hand.

He put her hand on his thigh. That was distracting. His thigh was as hard as rock. She thought he just sat at a computer all day, moving cattle around and sending sheep to market or whatever it was that cattlemen did to sheep. A Pig who had cattle and sheep. "Pig, what did your parents actually name you?"

"Colin."

"Colin?"

"You could call me Colly?"

A little disgruntled, Fred tried it out. "Colly and Fred. Fred and Colly. It sounds like a boy and his dog."

"You're no dog."

In disgust with him, she pointed out, "I'm the boy—"

But she didn't get to finish, because Colin snorted in disbelief. Then he ran his glance down her pale green dress in a way that made it disappear. He asked her, "Did your daddy give you permission to wear that outfit?"

That stirred her to a little revitalizing stimulation. "I'm thirty-three years old and my daddy doesn't tell me what to wear—or where to stay!'' She added that with her chin out. She was an independent woman, unlike that lily-livered Sheila who'd buckled down without even a token protest.

Colin looked down at her around his wide shoulder and said softly, ''Some man ought to take you in hand.''

The tone of his voice did weird things down inside the pit of her stomach. She squinted, trying to figure out why, and decided it was that new, soft way of speaking he'd acquired. ''I might allow Sling to have some say, but he appears a little distracted.'' She said that with her obedient hand captured against Colin's hard thigh.

''Yeah. Just a little distracted. But don't you fret. Four days of Natalie Comstock's supervision, and Sling, and smiling at the masses in this heat, will take their toll on Sheila. I figure by Sunday she'll start hankering for Oregon. You know Sling isn't the most stimulating person you've ever been around? And he doesn't verbalize. He might think she's pretty, but he won't think to mention it to her—several times a day.''

''Then he's a fool. Every woman wants to be told she's pretty.''

''You're not pretty.''

He didn't need to be so blunt. She knew that. ''I know.''

''You're ethereal. You're—''

Where'd he find that word? she wondered.

''—magic. You make my head spin.''

''Now, *that*'s the way a man should talk!'' She smiled at him delightedly. Then her smile slowly faded. ''Who have you told that to, to be so practiced?''

"Nobody. Nobody else." And his slow, sidelong look was so confidently male that she felt a little off-center. Then she remembered that underneath this new, smooth, hard man was really just Pig, whom she'd known forever.

When they all rose from the table and began to move around, preparing to go to the dance, Sling came up to Fred with firm intention. She smiled up at him. "Sling."

She'd said Sling's name in a voice that irritated the hell out of Colin.

Sling didn't particularly notice Colin's hostility, as he said to Fred, "I found a place for you and Pig at the Barretts' table. There just wasn't enough room at ours because Sheila had a whole list of people she wanted to see. I'm sorry, Fred. You will save me a dance?"

"His name is Colin." That's what came out of her mouth.

Sling blinked and asked, "Hmm?" leaning his head forward a little with the sound.

"Don't call him Pig, because his name is Colin."

Sling's surprised gaze lifted to Colin and he said "Is that so?" in some astonishment. "Colin, is it? I did wonder a time or two."

Entertained and just a tad smug that Fred would defend him, Colin asked, "When was that?"

"Oh, like riding fence lines. That sort of time when strange things come up and stick in your mind."

"Not when you were sloppin' the hogs?"

"Now you know I got no hogs. Colin. I'll have to remember that." Then he looked back at Fred and said seriously, "You do understand about the table and all this, don't you, Fred?"

No, she didn't understand, not one bit. But under the circumstances, what woman would say so? She looked at the beautiful Sling and her mouth said, "My name's Fredricka. I'm tired of being called Fred."

"You're starting a revolution here, aren't you, Fredricka. You always seemed such a peaceable woman." And Sling frowned a little at her, as if she'd surprised him.

At community functions, the Lamberts never sat together. They never had. Their daddy said he wanted to know all the gossip, so they had to spread out, sit at other tables and listen. They ought not to take notes too openly, but they weren't to forget anything.

None of the daughters was fooled. They knew he wanted to be with his friends and not have to be careful how he spoke. And he liked flirting with his wife. With all those daughters around him, he was reminded he was a little further down the years than he felt.

There was a five-dollar fine for any balloon that burst before eleven. After that, it was encouraged. But in the meantime, there were so many balloons in the meeting Hall that it was a little hard to get a clear view across the place. The Barretts were welcoming, and Fredricka mentioned that Pig's name was Colin. There were slight smiles and speaking glances exchanged, and everybody there was soon tripping over their tongues to remember to call Pig by his real name. They became devoted to changing their programmed tongues, to correcting each other.

Fredricka had chosen a good time to instigate the turnabout, since everyone was so avidly interested in Sheila being coupled with Fred's Sling.

When Fredricka realized she'd started an unstoppable change, she thought to ask Colin, "Did you want people to call you Colin?"

He laughed rather uproariously and was so loud that he sounded like the old Pig. His eyes were filled with his humor, and he watched her as he laughed.

She smiled a little, rather enjoying his boisterousness. "I suppose that you're implying it's too late to be asking your permission?"

He countered, "I was wondering why you didn't object to 'Pig' thirty years ago."

"I didn't notice."

"But now you do?" And his voice was back to that new softness.

"I like Colin."

"A Colin by any other name is still a Colin."

"That's true." She looked up at him for such a time that she wasn't aware of the regard they shared so soberly. But others at their table saw and exchanged looks with raised, questioning eyebrows.

It was just about a dance after that, still at the start of the evening, that Fredricka's new brothers-in-law came to their table and each introduced her to a "friend" who "just happened" to have come through the Texas Hill Country at that particular time. Colin observed this incredible coincidence with jaundiced eyes.

First was Quint. He brought over a very good-looking man of about thirty-five. Irish. Grinning. A delight. He was courteous and eager and asked Fredricka to dance. She looked at Colin, whose cool nod of permission suddenly became a little awed, and his lips parted. She'd asked *his* permission!

Well, of course, all the Lambert daughters had always done that with their dates. It was just that he'd never experienced it before then. It didn't mean anything. It was just a courtesy. When he'd asked Fredricka to dance at doings, she'd gotten Sling's permission. He watched as the new guy took Fredricka out onto the dance floor. The guy was selling. Cheerful, grinning, attentive, talking, questioning—selling.

When they got back to the table, Colin had a Barrett cousin lined up, and firmly sent Quint's man off to the dance floor with her.

Just then, Tate's Bill came along with a friend of his who just happened to be traveling through the Hill Country and came in time for the dance. He had the weekend free. Delighted, he grinned widely, his eyes busy on Fredricka, and he asked her to dance.

She looked at Colin, who took a deep breath and gave a brief jerk of a nod.

On the dance floor, Bill's friend asked, "He's a little territorial. You committed?"

Fredricka said, "Not to him."

Bill's friend said, "I don't believe he knows that."

And it didn't astonish Fredricka that when they got back to the table, Colin had a Comstock cousin waiting to meet Bill's friend.

So when Angus brought over a friend who was— and they all joined in, saying, "—just traveling through the Hill Country and—" everyone laughed and Colin found a Schmidt girl who was amiable.

But when Fredricka's daddy came over and introduced a magnificent man to her, there wasn't much Colin could do but glare at Jaff and be reluctant to let go of her arm.

On the dance floor, her daddy's contribution to the evening's entertainment of his daughter mentioned, "The way I heard it, you were languishing and snubbed. He doesn't look snubbing to me."

"That's Colin. It's Sling who is snubbing me. Who said I was being snubbed?"

"Your daddy. I'm a fourth cousin, and our particular branch of the family is out in New Mexico. That's how come we've never met, but most of my family have visited here. Remember Tom Poplar?"

"Kin to you?"

"Cousin."

She considered him intently, her mind working, then looked around before she accosted him. "You're a *cousin* to me, therefore you are obligated to assist. Kiss me."

"What?"

"Sling is looking this way," she said through her teeth. "Kiss me."

"Now, honey, I wouldn't mind kissing you for this Sling's benefit, but that Colin, over there, is about to breathe fire. He could *hit* me!"

Fred assured him, "If he hurt you, it would make me very angry."

"That wouldn't be a whole hell of a lot of help. For a woman who is supposed to be a wallflower, you look very involved. We had to wait three dances just so I could be introduced to you."

Fred threatened, "If you value your arches, kiss me right this minute! I demand it, as your cousin. There's the obligation of family loyalty. Do it."

"No. Being a Lambert back a ways did not make me foolish. That rock is coming over to cut in. Behave. My neck is precious to me."

She smiled unkindly. "I'm glad you all moved away. You're not even a real Texan, must less a Lambert."

Colin had another female in tow, and they traded partners just as Graham came along to introduce a fed who was stationed in Austin. Colin shook hands with the guy. "Glad you dropped by. I'm Colin Kilgallon. She's with me." Then he snared a passing Kilgallon relative as he growled in the fed's ear, "This one is taken. Try that one."

The fed looked a little startled, but Graham laughed out loud.

Fredricka waited until she and Colin had danced out of earshot, then she said, "You were a little rude to Graham's friend."

"Honey, you haven't seen rude. I was very, very careful. What was that guy saying to you—the one before this one—that made you mad?"

"I wanted him to kiss me, but he wouldn't. You scared him."

Steam came out of Colin's ears. "You wanted him to do—" he had to take a breath "—what?" And the word was said quite quietly.

"Sling was looking in our direction, and I thought if he saw that guy kiss me, it would attract Sling's attention." She looked up mutinously. "He wouldn't do it."

"Why not?"

"He was afraid of . . . you."

Colin looked around for the guy as he said, "Brighter than I thought. But why the hell were you asking some stranger to kiss you?"

"I've already told you. I wanted Sling to see another man kiss me."

"So you asked a total stranger to do it for you."

"Naw. He's a cousin from New Mexico. A branch of the Lamberts."

Colin looked at her. He knew his arms were too tight around her, and he was holding her too close. Then he growled, "All you had to do was ask."

Ask? She stared, vividly remembering the long-ago, shocking kiss Colin had given her in the dark, outside the gym. Slowly she said, "I need to comb my eyebrows." And she went off to the ladies' room to recover from the idea of Colin kissing her—again.

Five

While Fredricka was in the ladies' room "combing her eyebrows," Colin went around contacting her new brothers-in-law. He told them, "On the off chance that I could join your ranks how about calling off the strange dogs you brought in? If they keep on—and Quint, yours looks like he thinks I'm a challenge—I may have to arm wrestle them, and they look breakable." He spoke in that new, soft voice that was attention-getting.

His listeners exchanged amused glances of anticipation, and it was Bill who said, "They are all staying at the Lamberts'. The parents moved Jenny and Benjamin down to our room and us to the morning room."

Angus apologized: "With Jaff finding that cousin out in New Mexico, it would have been a six count, but one man I called couldn't make it. He wasn't reluctant, but his newly acquired live-in was opposed.''

Just thinking how that must have been, made them smile.

Leaving them, Colin hunted down Jaff Lambert. Referring to the New Mexico cousin who had intruded into the situation, Colin inquired a bit testily, ''Gathering the clan?''

''Did I misread the situation, Colin?''

The younger man nodded once to indicate Jaff had switched names for him, then he instructed, ''This is my main chance with Fredricka. Don't give me any more complications than I already have.''

''Good luck.'' Jaff grinned.

Somewhat disgruntled, Colin grated, ''That's nice to hear.''

''I believe I ought to tell you we did it more to stimulate you than Sling. He's never been a real contender. It's just that Fredricka hasn't realized that.''

Colin gave a nod of agreement. ''Quint's man tends to look on this as a diversion. I won't be able to be hospitable to your guest.''

''All's fair,'' Jaff quoted, then he added: ''Try not to break up the furniture.''

Colin grinned, and Jaff laughed and patted the younger man's shoulder.

So the decks were cleared and all that Colin really had to contend with was Fredricka's lack of perception. She had a case of tunnel vision that had nothing to do with sight. He had to show her a broader view—him.

Since Colin was a musician, he knew rhythm and his body loved it, so he danced well. He danced with

Fredricka; and being a gentleman, he showed her off, guiding her to being better than she really was.

On the other hand, Sling was no dancer at all. All he did was clutch the woman and shuffle. Women *loved* to dance with Sling. They loved to be clutched against him and shuffle. Sling came and claimed his dance with Fredricka, and Colin died. He watched with darkened eyes and tensed muscles and hated every minute.

Fredricka enjoyed being clutched against Sling.

Sling talked. He said, "Poor Sheila. She's having a tough time of it. She needs someone to talk to."

"You," Fredricka guessed.

"We were very close that last year of high school. She doesn't have your self-confidence. You're really a very secure woman."

This so astonished Fredricka that she was silent as Sling went on about Sheila's loneliness and lack of self-worth.

Fredricka struggled to believe that, as Sheila sparkled all over the dim Hall.

Watching Sling and Fredricka dance, Colin thought how amazing—Sling was out there with Fredricka clutched against him, and he could *talk*! It gradually dawned on Colin that maybe Sling wasn't in love with Fredricka. Maybe he just was nice, kind. And his niceness and kindness had been misinterpreted by Fredricka to mean that he really could love her.

Colin wondered: Now, how was he going to tell that to Fredricka? She thought she loved Sling. Colin couldn't just blurt out that Sling didn't love her; she'd be crushed. She wasn't too confident in herself, anyway. Look at that dress she was wearing that was setting all the guys' eyes to spinning. A confident woman wouldn't wear that kind of dress. So Fredricka didn't need him telling her the truth about Sling. It would devastate her. This conveyance of the facts would need to be very delicately done. He worried that she could be hurt. And he hated it that Sling was out there on the floor holding her as he held every other woman, but Fredricka would think Sling was holding her that way because he loved her.

Or did he?

Colin debated. Could he be deluding himself into thinking Sling didn't love Fredricka because he didn't want Sling as competition? As always, Colin took out the memory of that kiss he'd given Fredricka in the dark, outside the gym all those years ago. He'd worn Sling's hat and jacket, and he'd kissed Fredricka just the way he'd longed to, and she'd responded so wildly that he *almost* couldn't stop it. It had about wrecked him. No other woman had touched his senses or his soul the way Fredricka had. And if she would just admit it, it had been the same for her.

Colin knew the only problem he had was in getting her to recognize the truth. There were little clues that he was right. Did she realize she was protective of him? Just tonight she was turning everyone to calling him by his real name. It was going to take him a while to get used to answering to it.

And there was the fact of that long-ago kiss. That was all he really needed. But he'd had on Sling's hat and jacket and she'd thought the kiss was for Sling. He'd watched that pair kiss, and he would swear she'd never responded to Sling the way she had to him that night by the gym. Then she had responded to the *man*. She'd only *thought* it was to that hat and jacket of Sling.

She did remember the kiss. Just look how she'd run from the idea of kissing him again. She'd looked so startled when he'd offered to kiss her for Sling's benefit that she'd skedaddled off to the ladies' room. And with Sling's turn on the dance floor finished, she went along with a couple of women to the ladies' room again.

In that dark, noisy, crowded Hall, Colin shifted in his chair, waiting for Fredricka to come back to him. He could surely give her ample opportunity to make Sling jealous. He put his hand over his mouth in a slouching, bored way, but it was to hide the little smile that he couldn't prevent at the idea of what he could do to try to make Sling jealous. And since Colin was almost positive that Sling couldn't possibly *be* jealous of Fredricka, it might take some doing. His body tingled down its length and he got up and moved around, keeping the ladies' room door in sight.

She finally emerged with a covey of friends. Colin went to meet her; and she smiled. He asked, "Would you like a drink? We could go out to the car."

Liquor wasn't allowed inside the Hall. Colin thought that was an interesting division of rules. It was all right in cars. In Texas, driving while drinking wasn't illegal. There were even drive-through beer stops. But the ruling ladies had banned liquor inside the Hall.

Fredricka looked around the Hall and Sling was nowhere in sight. He was out in one of the cars with Sheila? She said to Colin, "Okay." But remembering her conduct at the rodeo, she added, "No beer."

They went out into the mild night with its gentle Gulf breeze. The stars were billions and billions. No one else was outside that she could see. That made her feel she was being a little bold.

Colin took her hand and led her to his car. He smiled in the starlight. "Sure you don't want a beer? I have Lone Star and Pearl. Or rum and Coke? Or gin and tonic?"

"My word! You have a whole bar." She made conversation. "I'll have a rum and Coke." She'd never been so intimately situated with...Colin—alone, standing by his car with him. "I don't see Sling's pickup."

"They went to move Sheila's things to the Comstocks'."

"Oh."

He saw that she looked defeated. Could he allow that? No. He was doomed to be honest. "Of course, Natalie Comstock sent her daughter along. Propriety, you must realize, comes before everything else. Lizzabelle was furious to be dragged away from the dance." It killed Colin to see Fredricka brighten.

"Lizzabelle will see to it that the move is accomplished with dispatch." She smiled sharingly.

"Sling looks good on the outside, but underneath he's really a selfish bachelor," Colin instructed gently. "He likes his own way. With people, he just tags along. He isn't an instigator. When he does marry, it won't be because he thought of it." That ought to give her something to think about.

She did look thoughtful as she studied the beautiful Texas night. Then she turned to Colin and exclaimed, "Thank you. That helps. You mean I should propose to him."

"No!"

"But you just said—"

He'd just said too damn much! "If you're a smart woman, you'll wait until you see some sign that he is ready. Sling isn't at all ready to marry yet. He's only thirty-three. He's spent all these years getting his scrambled life organized, what with being responsible for all that tribe of his. He'll want some time to survey his accomplishments before he looks around and complicates hisself again in taking a wife. Just the very *peace* now is fascinating him."

Dangerously calm, Fredricka inquired gently, "You believe a wife complicates a man's life?"

Colin opened his busy mouth and managed not to say anything until he came up with "Did I say that?"

She gave one very stiff nod of her head and replied, "You said he was enjoying the peace before he compli-cates his life with a wife."

"Hey, that rhymes! Life and wife. Uh…listen. I like that piece. Hear it? Let's get back inside and dance. If you're not going to drink that, put it there for later." He indicated the dashboard. "Hustle up. The piece will be over."

So they got inside the Hall at the beginning of the next number, and they ran right into Quint's man, who smiled real big at Colin and asked Fredricka to dance.

Colin took Fredricka's arm in his hand and put the other out to ward off the intruder. He said, "Run along before you lose all your marbles." And he said it nasty.

Quint's man laughed. That raised Colin's hackles. And the look in the intruder's eyes was one that noted and enjoyed it. Colin said in the new, soft way, "I have a bottle in my car. Would you care for a drink?" It wasn't a cordial invitation, it was a threatening one, asking the man to step outside and discuss his conduct.

The intruder laughed again. "I'll pass—this time."

Back in the ladies' room, Fredricka reported that conversation to Hillary and Tate. She had waited for Georgina to leave first, since Quint was her husband, and Fredricka didn't want to sound critical of a friend of her sister's husband. When she'd finished telling them about that intruder, Fredricka had to wait until both sisters quit laughing before she said in a toplofty voice, "I don't believe you all remember that Colin does have something of a temper."

Tate hastened to say, "We weren't laughing at Colin. We just think it's typical of any man Quintus Finnig would know. From what Georgina tells us, Quint knows people all over the country, and they are as unmoving and as loyal and as different as Quint Finnig. Maybe you ought to tell Colin to back off from Quint's friend. He is a guest. And he'll be staying at our house this weekend."

"Okay. I'll tell him."

But when she did, Colin just put his hand on Fredricka's nape and shook her a little as he replied, "Don't worry your pretty little head about me."

"I'm not worrying about *you*. You can take care of yourself. But that guy's going to be at our house, and he *is* a guest, and I'd hate for you to bloody him up. I can dance with the guy. There's no harm in that. He's a family guest and in this crowded Hall, I won't be seduced or molested. It's a simple dance in a place where I know just about every single person."

Colin looked at Fredricka standing there so earnest and sincere. So she thought he could take care of himself? He was torn between pride and irritation.

Why couldn't she worry about what could happen to him? Any yahoo that stood up to Colin Kilgallon—in person—was no pansy. Quint's friend could undoubtedly handle himself just great. He probably fought dirty. "Don't leave the Hall."

"Why would I leave the Hall?" She was entirely reasonable.

He looked at her darkly. "You might want a drink."

She flung out her arms and said in annoyance, "I don't need one. If I did, there's still that one in your car."

"Don't go out of the Hall without me."

Not showing any patience at all, the wimp replied, "I won't, I won't, I won't! Okay?" She stormed off through the bodies that were packed in there, along with all the balloons, and found Quint's friend. They danced. Colin watched from under his shaggy pale eyebrows.

Tate's Bill came along and asked Colin politely, "Lovers' quarrel?"

Colin muttered, "I wish."

Bill grinned and sympathized. "From what I know and gather from my fellows-in-law, these Lambert women are worth the bother. Good luck."

"Tell Quint to call him off."

Bill replied, "His name's Vinnie. He has charmed Ethel. He's here for the duration."

"Goody," Colin commented stonily.

Bill explained, "It'll stimulate you."

"I may stimulate him right out of that house."

"Now you know you can't do that," Bill chided. "Ethel and Jaff would be disapproving. That's no way to start a relationship. Just be patient."

"I have this weekend to begin convincing Fredricka. I don't need any Vinnie horning in."

Bill watched Colin for a minute. Then he said, "You can count on me."

They shook hands.

Colin got Fredricka back when the dance was over, and she was a little surprised by the look he exchanged with Vinnie, and she wasn't sure she liked Vinnie's laugh. It sounded as if he had flipped a ball into a basket or something. She gave Vinnie a diminishing glance and went with Colin. Colin was home folks and one never allowed an intruder to score against one's own.

In the course of that ragged evening, another one of Fredricka's new brothers-in-law told Colin pretty much the same thing that Bill had: Colin could count on them for whatever aid he might need. And Georgina's Quint shook his head in apology and explained, "With these guys, you give'em an order and they do it even if the order's canceled. See? I'll be around watching'em. You watch Fredricka."

Colin didn't know exactly what Quint meant by "these guys," but he believed he did. He'd heard Quint Finnig had a smoky background. It couldn't be Mafia, because these men were all Irish. But everyone knew Irishmen were loyal—to the death. That might mean Vinnie was like a pit bulldog. Colin took a deep, enduring breath. Fredricka was worth whatever it took.

In the progressively noisier crowd that night, with trips out to cars, Angus said to Colin, "You and your struggles have heightened my interest in this weekend considerably." He added the explanation: "I had to leave perfect sailing weather on Lake Michigan to come down here.''

Colin could see the man was no Texan. The weather was perfect there in Texas. With that good land, you didn't need to get on water to appreciate the day. ''You can go over to Lake Medina. That's just southeast of here and less than fifty miles. Or you can go east toward San Marcos, to the reservoir, or a bit over fifty miles up to Marble Falls. You don't need the whole of Lake Michigan, so there'd be room enough. I got some friends with sailboats, so I can fix you up, whichever way you want to go. Say the word.''

Angus nodded. ''I'd appreciate it.''

''And you can fish,'' Colin added.

''I'd just like to sail. It would be nice to get out.''

Colin inquired, ''You ride a horse?''

Angus shook his head.

''Wanna learn?''

Angus grinned. ''Not this time. My business is boats. You probably feel the same about horses.''

''Riding's as free as sailing, and your 'boat' is as interested as you. It's a fine way to see the land—from the back of a horse.''

''I'd like that another time. Give me a rain check.''

And Colin promised, ''You got it.''

''And may I offer may assistance in whatever capacity you might need me?'

Colin put out his hand. ''Now I am obliged. My thanks.''

Fredricka was approaching and both men turned to watch her. She asked, ''What are you plotting that you'd shake hands in just that way?''

Quite easily, Colin replied, ''I'm fixing Angus up to go sailing.''

Fredricka looked critically at Hillary's husband. "Homecomings bore you?"

Colin confided to Angus: "That's Fredricka's example of tact."

Although he smiled, Angus told her, "I believe if it's your school or your community, it's more interesting."

She could see that. "Sail tomorrow, because on Sunday we have to all go to church so the older generation can see the crop of sons-in-law that the Lambert daughters snared."

Angus demurred. "It's nice of you to say it that way, but I had to work my, uh, self to a bone to attract Hillary. It was I who 'snared' her."

Patently unbelieving, Fredricka nodded.

After Angus went back to Hillary, Fredricka told Colin, "He thinks he snared Hillary. Did you know she went into the wrong apartment and he found her in his bed?"

"Men have a hard time." Colin sighed as he said the words.

"Baloney."

He gave her a lazy look and suggested, "Let's go out to the car and drink that drink. I'm about to die of the heat."

"Sling and Sheila aren't back yet."

"Maybe she had furniture."

Soberly Fredricka glanced coldly at him and said, "That's very funny."

Outside in the cool air, Colin flapped his jacket and rounded his lips to blow out scorching air. But Fredricka was chilled. He gladly removed his jacket as he lowered his lashes to covertly watch her nipples, peaked by her chill; and he very tenderly put the heated jacket around her shoulders.

She pulled its warmth close around her, saying "Umm," and she closed her eyes.

Colin considered all the ways he could warm her, all the ways to elicit that sound from her. All—

"Do you have to travel this week?"

"No." He wondered at her question.

"I hadn't realized how much traveling your place takes. Daddy doesn't go out nearly as much as you. He mostly just goes to see if he can find a mean horse to ride."

Colin realized she was flawed. Having grown up there, knowing all the people who lived around that area, did she think he *really* needed to travel that much for his place? He'd gone to see her. He'd just let her think it was a happenstance, that he'd had business near where she had been. "One of these days your daddy is going to break his neck on some dumb horse."

"Momma worries about that. But he loves it. There aren't many ways a man can test himself and enjoy it so. Momma says there's a flaw in Daddy that he seems to need the risk. She sweats blood, but she's never yet mentioned that to Daddy."

"Maybe she should." So the flaw came from her daddy's side. That figured. When he and Fredricka had their kids, that flaw would probably pop up in some of them. He thought of the flaws, then of the children, then of making babies with her.

In concern, she told him, "You look odd. Are you all right?"

She could worry about him? So he explained with contrived calculation, "I was just wondering if that Vinnie might get nasty."

"The reason I danced with him was to feel his muscles. He can't match you. I kept him away very easi—"

"What'd he try?" Colin snapped

"Nothing! Some people dance close. Like Sling. He has to dance close because he can't dance—Not really. He has no rhythm—"

Colin was *astounded* she knew that.

"—like Sling. But it was no trouble countering it."

Colin's attention had gotten back to her a little late and he had to figure out what she was saying was, that Vinnie had tried to hold her close and she hadn't allowed it. That made Colin very mellow. She had let him hold her close but not Vinnie. He said huskily, "You should kiss me good-night now."

"You're leaving?"

"No. But when I take you home there will be all your sisters and their husbands and your momma and daddy, and I won't get a decent kiss if I get any at all."

She parried, "Why should I kiss you?"

He knew from her question that she was nervous. Good. That meant she didn't consider him like a cousin or just a neighbor. He explained, "Because all ladies do that for the escort. It makes taking the ladies around worthwhile for a man. It's an endurance, taking a woman to dances and things. But the idea of a kiss helps get a man through the evening."

"If I'd known what a chore it was, I could have driven myself."

He sighed. "I may throttle you."

With a bit of sauciness she retorted, "I suppose that would save me from kissing you."

In that new, soft way, he told her positively: "You like kissing me. Don't fool yourself. Come on."

She said slowly, "Sling—"

"You don't love Sling. The only reason you thought you did was because there isn't a whole lot of choice around these parts, and he *is* a prize. You're just wrestling with the Lambert competitiveness."

"You're the only one who thinks I'm competitive. Everybody in the family thinks I'm a wimp."

"You're a tiger and—"

But headlights swept around and Sling's pickup came into the parking area with Sheila and a disgruntled Lizzabelle. Lizzabelle got out of the truck and gave Fredricka a tightly held, speaking glance that showed her patience was very worn. Then Lizzabelle went off to the Hall without a word.

The golden light that was Sheila bounced out of Sling's pickup as Colin held the door, while Sling slowly crawled out the other side. He didn't smile.

Therefore Fredricka asked brightly, "All moved?" and waited with an interested smile.

As Sheila chittered away in an elaborately vivacious rendering of their adventures, Colin put a hand on Fredricka's nape and tightened his grip enough to catch her attention. In her ear, Colin just barely breathed, "Leave it."

Seeing the situation was eruptive, and still bent-nosed from being pushed aside, Fredricka was so sorely tempted to push the whole mess to explosion for her own satisfaction that she had one hell of a struggle. She even turned a laughing-eyed plea to Colin. He watched her intently, so avidly, that when he re-

FIRST-CLASS ROMANCE

Mail This Heart TODAY!

And We'll Deliver:

**4 FREE BOOKS
A FREE DIGITAL CLOCK/CALENDAR
PLUS
A SURPRISE MYSTERY BONUS
TO YOUR DOOR!**

See Inside For More Details

SILHOUETTE DELIVERS FIRST-CLASS ROMANCE— DIRECT TO YOUR DOOR

Mail the Heart sticker on the postpaid order card today and you'll receive:

—4 new Silhouette Desire® novels—FREE
—a lovely lucite digital clock/calendar—FREE
—and a surprise mystery bonus—FREE

But that's not all. You'll also get:

Free Home Delivery

When you subscribe to Silhouette Desire®, the excitement, romance and faraway adventures of these novels can be yours for previewing in the convenience of your own home. Every month we'll deliver 6 new books right to your door. If you decide to keep them, they'll be yours for only $2.24* each—that's 26 cents below the cover price, and there is *no* extra charge for postage and handling! There is no obligation to buy— you can cancel at any time simply by writing ''cancel'' on your statement or by returning a shipment of books to us at our cost.

Free Monthly Newsletter

It's the indispensable insider's look at our most popular writers and their upcoming novels. Now you can have a behind-the-scenes look at the fascinating world of Silhouette! It's an added bonus you'll look forward to every month!

Special Extras—FREE

Because our home subscribers are our most valued readers, we'll be sending you additional free gifts from time to time in your monthly book shipments as a token of our appreciation.

OPEN YOUR MAILBOX TO A WORLD OF LOVE AND ROMANCE EACH MONTH. JUST COMPLETE, DETACH AND MAIL YOUR FREE-OFFER CARD TODAY!

*Terms and prices subject to change without notice. Sales tax applicable in N.Y. and Iowa.
© 1989 HARLEQUIN ENTERPRISES LIMITED

FREE! lucite digital clock/calendar

You'll love your digital clock/calendar!
The changeable month-at-a-glance calendar
pops out and can be replaced with your
favorite photograph. It is yours FREE as
our gift of love!

Silhouette 🖤 Desire®

FREE OFFER CARD

4 FREE BOOKS

**FREE DIGITAL
CLOCK/CALENDAR**

**FREE MYSTERY
BONUS**

PLACE
HEART
STICKER
HERE

**FREE HOME
DELIVERY**

**FREE FACT-FILLED
NEWSLETTER**

**MORE SURPRISES
THROUGHOUT THE
YEAR—FREE**

✓ **YES!** Please send me four Silhouette Desire®
novels, free, along with my free digital clock/
calendar and my free mystery gift as explained on the
opposite page.

225 CIS JAY6
(U-S-D-11/89)

NAME _____

ADDRESS _____ APT. _____

CITY _____ STATE _____

ZIP CODE _____

Offer limited to one per household and not
valid to current Silhouette Desire®
subscribers. All orders subject
to approval. Terms and prices
subject to change
without notice.

MAIL THE POSTPAID CARD TODAY!

SILHOUETTE "NO RISK" GUARANTEE
There is no obligation to buy—the free books and gifts remain yours to keep. You receive
books before they're available in stores. You may end your subscription anytime—just write
"cancel" on your statement or return your shipment of books at our cost.

© 1989 HARLEQUIN ENTERPRISES LIMITED

PRINTED IN U.S.A.

Remember! To receive your free books, digital clock/calendar and mystery gift, return the postpaid card below. But don't delay!

DETACH AND MAIL CARD TODAY.

MAIL THE POSTPAID CARD TODAY!

BUSINESS REPLY CARD

FIRST CLASS MAIL   PERMIT NO. 717   BUFFALO, NY

POSTAGE WILL BE PAID BY ADDRESSEE

SILHOUETTE BOOKS
901 FUHRMANN BLVD
PO BOX 1867
BUFFALO NY 14240-9952

NO POSTAGE
NECESSARY
IF MAILED
IN THE
UNITED STATES

sponded to the humor in her, there was answering laughter in his eyes.

Colin said to Sling, "How about a bracing drink before you face the mob."

Sheila bubbled, "Are they all drunk?"

"They're not even trying," Colin replied lazily as he handed Sling a bottle of Scotch. "I think you've forgotten how seldom we all get together and how stimulating and joyful company can be."

Sling took one careful mouthful of Colin's Scotch and stood with it in his mouth, and he looked off into the silent night before he slowly swallowed.

Sheila was sharing the joys of returning home. And she was carefully regretful she'd had to be moved that night over to Mrs. Comstock's house. It had been such a nuisance.

Fredricka watched Sling, wondering what had happened, while Colin looked at Sheila.

"You know, Colin, I don't really remember you from all those years ago. You're older, but I can't imagine how I don't remember you." She smiled at him to make up for that oversight.

Fredricka heard that tone. The words were okay, it was that wheedling tone. Sheila wasn't missing any bets. She was casting lures to Colin? Indignation swelled in Fredricka's chest and she gasped as she turned to stare at this malignancy.

Colin's chest, too, swelled—but with excitement. He, too, heard the lure in Sheila's tone, but what his ears soaked up, and what spread through his body like warm honey, was Fredricka's gasp. So he smiled a little.

With that smile, Sheila turned full wattage on her new admirer. Then she slowly turned and gave Fredricka a measuring look that made Fredricka lift her chin in challenge—and a *great* deal of curiosity. What had happened? It was four very introspective people who went back into the Hall.

Inside those concrete blocks, the noise was deafening. It was a whole lot worse after eleven when the balloons were being popped. By then, most of the more conservative people had left, and only the hardcore party people were still there. Sheila was relentlessly so. Sling was almost asleep.

Sheila came over to the Barrett table and enthused: "Come on over to our table, there's room now."

But Colin replied, "We're in the midst of a big discussion."

Brightly, Sheila replied, "Then the mountain will come to Muhammad."

Sling was pried up and moved, and he came to lounge by Fredricka, silent and sleepy. Sheila moved next to Colin to join in the discussion about how to keep cattle yards from polluting the groundwater. Since Colin held Fredricka's hand and didn't change the subject, Sheila was silent. But there were those who came and took her away to dance, and who stood around and laughed with her and admired her. Fredricka saw Sheila maneuvered so that she was always nearby, allowing Sling to see her popularity. Or was she trying to impress Colin?

When the time came to leave the Hall, almost everyone trailed out into the parking lot, still stimulated and visiting. It was then that Sheila admired Colin's little green car, which was such a trial to get into and out again. Then Fredricka realized Sheila was telling Sling that she didn't much care to be carted around in a pickup truck.

While Sheila was gushing away over the little car, Colin slowly removed his suit jacket and slung it into the nothing backseat. He stepped aside and helped Fredricka lower herself into the machine, and with Sheila still talking, Colin walked around and got in on the other side. He started the motor as Sheila waved goodbye, then he backed away and drove toward the Lambert home. On the way, Colin stopped the little car on a deserted side road and requested that Fredricka kiss him good-night.

She laughed. "You didn't forget!"

"Not likely."

She turned her head and looked at him, reminding herself that he was still just Pig, not a stranger whom she needed to be wary about. He was a friend. So she scooted over to the edge of the bucket seat, and she reached a hand to lay it along the side of his cheek.

But Colin released her seat belt, turned her, and with an expertise that slipped away into one of Fredricka's mental cracks, he put his hands under her armpits, lifted and shifted her until she lay slanted across his chest. Then he looked into her eyes, very seriously, before he lowered his head and . . . he really kissed her.

It was no "good-night" kiss. It was a full-blown, magnificent sexual mating of their mouths. It was spectacular! Fredricka's insides quivered erotically, with thrills licking along in secret places. Her skin's surface was exquisitely aware of her stockings, her garter belt, the silken caress of her panties. The inside of her stomach shivered, and her breasts were conscious they were squashed against the hard wall of Colin's chest. His mouth tasted different from any man's mouth she'd ever known, and her tongue relished it. He kissed differently. She was so stunningly aware that it was Colin kissing her, and it was the same as that shocking time in the dark, outside the gym. No mistake this time, it was Colin.

All of her senses were tremblingly alert. She noted his hard hands were very large and covered a great deal of her side and that his thumb was pressing into the side of her sensitive and excessively alert breast. Her knees couldn't be still, and her hands were up in his carroty hair instead of down moving his hands back where they belonged. Her eyelids were so very heavy, and her neck wasn't strong. That didn't matter, because he pushed her weighty head over against his shoulder and she sighed into his mouth, making him groan.

But then he put his hands back under her arms and lifted her boneless body back over into the passenger seat! She was stunned, until he put his fists on top of the steering wheel and lay his forehead on them and panted with his mouth open.

Concerned, she questioned, "Colin?"

"You are a dangerous woman. It's just like it was before."

So he, too, remembered that kiss by the gym! How embarrassing.

Six

Colin didn't touch Fredricka again. He got out of the car and walked around, acting as if he were having trouble moving and breathing, as if he were hurting. He rubbed his chest and once he tried to lift the car. He was very strange. She'd never in her life seen a man behave that way.

Then he got back into the driver's seat and sat, staring ahead, before he took a deep, careful breath. He started the car, and they drove in silence. While Fredricka was bug-eyed over her adventurously riotous response to a man, Colin took occasional deep breaths, blowing them out as he shook his head.

Fredricka realized Colin was fighting for control. To her knowledge, Sling had never reacted in this way to any of their kisses. Of course, neither had she. But it was a little awesome that she could set Colin on his ear that way. It was tempting to see if it would happen again. But she wasn't sure what sort of power that might unleash. She hadn't been in control of herself. It had been Colin who had put her aside so firmly. What if he hadn't?

The thought boggled her—and beckoned to her. What would have happened? Well, obviously it was a good thing he'd stopped them. She hadn't. Why had he?

So?

Just what was she toying with, thinking that way? Well…she was curious. She'd never seen a man in the powerful grip of sexual need. That's what had swept through them. But Colin had recognized it and prevented anything from happening. He had protected her from his lust. So why was she annoyed with him? Did she want Colin to… Well, to be… Did she want . . . Colin?

Maybe so.

How surprising. Not really. She'd wanted him once before, in the darkness outside the gym. He'd stopped then, too. She could understand it then, but why had he stopped just now? He could have kissed her again. She'd liked it. It was like being in a soft, caressing, sensual sea of eroticism. She'd never paid that much attention to herself as being a woman, but with his kiss, she was not only aware of her femininity, she wanted Colin aware of it.

Inside the car there was no sound but the soft hum of the engine of that sexy little car. Out of the corners of her eyes, Fredricka peeked at Colin. He wasn't quite as tall as Sling. He wasn't as slim, either; he was a little bulkier. His fingers weren't as long as Sling's. His were thicker. His palms were rough. They'd rasped on the silk of that pale green dress as they'd moved on her body, feeling her so scandalously.

Her breasts tautened and her nipples hardened and a flight of something like awareness skittered over her skin's surface, making her very conscious of her body in a strange way. A different way. She wanted him to stop the car and...and...kiss her again.

She looked out the window at the black night rushing past almost soundlessly. He'd been right to stop them and to put her aside. She needed time to figure out why she had this explosive reaction to Colin, whom she'd known all her life with no marked reaction, except for just two times.

Maybe she was a dormant sex maniac. Only he could awaken this magic, uh, this curse that lurked in her. If she was fully awakened she would go berserk and no man would be safe from her. Well, Vinnie would be. And...Vinnie? Maybe he wouldn't! She'd never known she was susceptible to Colin. To Pig? She was susceptible to a man who'd spent most of his life being called Pig. In that case, was Vinnie safe? How about the others?

What horror had Colin stirred into wakening? Her lust could burst free and she'd prowl the countryside, seducing unsuspecting, unwilling men. She would have to be careful. She shouldn't be responsible for corrupting anyone else.

She peeked again from the corners of her eyes. Maybe it wasn't she who was lustful; maybe it was *Colin* who was the corrupter! She'd never been this way with any other man who'd kissed her, and in thirty-three years, she'd kissed her share. *It was COLIN!*

Of course! It was he who was the seducer. He who made sex seem so alluring, so urgent. He who was so vibrantly sexual that he infected her with the lustfulness. He'd probably ruined her.

Then a thought occurred: after kissing Colin, and knowing it *was* Colin who had made her feel that madness, could she go back to Sling's pleasant kisses?

No.

She was ruined.

She sighed rather sadly. She had a choice. She could have a nice, safe, sedate life with Sling, or a wild, mad, erotic collision with Colin. She smiled and slid another kind of look over at Colin sitting over there, driving the car up her parents' lane. He'd won.

He saw that look and almost hit the mulberry, then he had to dodge a crepe myrtle. He took his paralyzed foot off the gas and coasted to a stop. He looked back at her and she looked perfectly normal—as normal as a woman like Fredricka could look. Had he mistaken her glance? She'd looked like a siren. It must have been the light.

Then she leaned over and offered her lips. He kissed her cautiously. She smiled—her eyelids a little heavy—and she asked, "Where are you escorting me next?"

He couldn't breathe. Did she know what she was saying? He'd told her men took women around to doings so they could get kisses. Did she want another of *his* kisses? Did she mean that? "Do you mean that?"

She nodded.

With the nod, he realized that she did know what he'd meant. She was inviting him to escort her again and she knew it would cost her a kiss. Okay.

He almost couldn't get out of the car and walk around to open her door to help her out. But a man could do what he had to do. He said to her in that new, low voice of his: "Behave yourself."

She raised her eyebrows just a sassy bit and smiled almost not at all—just like a teasing woman who knew she was doing it—as she gave him a questioning look.

He growled, "Until I tell you otherwise."

So he did understand that she was willing to tussle. Or at least to test the waters. She studied him for a slight weighing time, then she said, "Good night." And she walked on over to the porch steps, knowing he was still standing there, watching her. She'd never had a man watch after her, not that she knew, and she liked it.

She paused inside the door and watched as Colin got back into his car and drove it off down the lane. She turned then, and followed the sounds to the kitchen where some sisters, some brothers-in-law and some guests of brothers-in-law were eating sandwiches or cake or pie. They were talking, gesturing, laughing. She smiled and closed the door to go up the steps where there were those who lounged in the hall to discuss and gesture.

Fredricka lifted a friendly hand to acknowledge any who might glance up, before she went into her room and closed her door. She was tired, but there was a strange exhilaration in her. She went to the window to smile out at the night, then went to her mirror to lean close and smile at herself. She walked around with her mind fluttery and drunk with new sensations, wanting to try kissing Colin again.

She slept heavily, pleasantly, restfully.

Colin did not.

* * *

Saturday was a day chock-full of events that gar-
nered very little real civic enthusiasm. Fredricka
sighed. But when one was a member of such a small
community, there was no choice but to be supportive.
The archery competition was at nine that morning.

Colin came by for Fredricka in plenty of time, and
they did go. The area was very loyal, so there were
people around, and it wasn't necessary for the pair to
line up and yell louder in order to make up for those
not present.

Sling and Sheila were there, being King and Queen
of the whole weekend. Fredricka groused to Colin,
"How can she look so... vibrant at this hour, and for
archery?"

In that new, quiet way of speaking that he'd taken
up, Colin gave the logical reply: "She's been up there
in Oregon's moist coolness that makes women's com-
plexions so pretty and soft. She's riding free on that
stored moisture. She's no longer used to our Texas air
that's so nice and dry. In four days, she'll look like an
old, empty, leather saddlebag that was abandoned out
in the desert some time back." He watched Sheila,
then added. "She wants to be admired, but Sling never
got the habit." Then he slid his fingers into the back
pockets of his jeans and turned to Fredricka. "You
like being admired?"

She shrugged. "I've never known anyone to admire me."

He tried not to laugh.

"It's true." She was a little indignant. "People are
nice to me, but they stand away from me. No one ever
tries to be friends."

"That right?"

She frowned at Colin. "You asked and I've replied. Now you want to know if I'm telling the truth?"

"Well, I can understand people not wanting to stand right next to you be— Now, just a minute, Fredricka, let me finish! If they should stand right next to you, then it's too obvious when they stare at you, but if they're standing a little away from you, then they can pretend to look around, or beyond you, and sneak in some stares at you."

"I'm that peculiar?" she groused.

Gently, he replied, "You're that beautiful."

She looked up, disgusted, knowing he was laughing at her, but his face was completely serious. So serious that the sun-squinted, untanned fan-lines around his eyes were white in his sun-browned face. A little breathless, she told Colin, "No one has ever told me that I am pretty—"

"Beautiful," he corrected.

Very pleased, she blushed in a charming way.

He explained, "They probably thought you already knew."

"My sisters are all so gorgeous."

He nodded as he maneuvered her among those loyal archery spectators. "Your sisters are routinely beautiful; you're uniquely so."

"Oh, Colin, you're so sweet."

"Now that's something that I do know. I'm a darling man, but with you, I'm an honest one. I'd never try to fool you. And you can count on me to tell you the truth. I might shade it a bit for somebody else, but I will always give it to you straight."

"I do appreciate you, Colin." She looked up to smile at him, and he tilted his head down as he looked toward her. From under the brim of his Stetson, the look he gave her was so different that her lips parted in a little gasp and a shivery quiver touched along inside her. She looked ahead, and it was just a good thing that Colin was guiding her, because she couldn't focus.

Fredricka did surface when she realized Sheila was coaxing Colin to let her and Sling ride in Colin's little car.

Sling objected. "That matchbox isn't big enough. My pickup's fine."

Sheila was almost sharp as she countered, "It makes my teeth rattle."

Sling was unperturbed. "Beats walking."

So only Fredricka rode with Colin over to the fishing contest. There was a little more interest there, a larger crowd.

The Weidmeyers' pond had been stocked with trout. The banks held shouldering fisherpeople, and Colin saw that tangled lines were a problem. It was interesting to see how different personalities handled lines that someone else had snarled.

Sheila was one of those fishing. She was giggling and being noticeable. Sling watched the others as he slouched along, talking to most of those who were just observing.

Colin said of Sling, "He'd be a great politician."

"Doing what?"

"Sheriff or mayor. People like him. He's a fine man. Ask him to do things for the community, and he will. He's the only man around here who had the guts to back the ballet without having any snickering done."

"You could have," Fredricka assured him.

"Among the boys, there would have been snickers, even about me. The ballet has been a great widening of knowledge and appreciation not only for the kids, but for those 'boys.' They've had the opportunity to see what beautiful athletes ballet dancers have to be...and the music. Sling has enriched all our lives. He's so secure, nothing can touch him because he doesn't care if people approve of him or not."

Fredricka looked at Colin in surprise. "But *you* care whether or not people approve of you?"

"I'm a lonely guy."

She hooted laughter.

But he was serious. "I am. Look at me."

She took his arm and leaned her head briefly against his shoulder as she laughed at such a man being lonely.

So she missed the fact that he was serious.

The fishing wasn't finished by lunchtime. At the concession, which the committee had provided for profit, the pair were among others who bought chips along with hot dogs dripping mustard and pickle relish. Colin again coaxed Fredricka to try another beer, but she ignored his attempt at her corruption and chose lemonade.

It was while Colin and Fredricka were munching the hot dogs that most of the rest of the Lambert household arrived. All of Fredricka's sisters came with their husbands, the two children with some Lambert cousins their ages, and of course, the Lambert houseguests. Of those, Quint's guest Vinnie was one.

The Lambert household members all greeted one another and had comments. It was Vinnie who said to Fredricka, "You didn't wait for me."

"I'm not your hostess," she reminded him.

"But everyone in the house is supposed to see to a guest's comfort and entertainment," he replied in a very sassily amused way. "You've been neglecting me."

"I thought one of the Barretts had her fingernails in you."

"She's a fine girl." Vinnie smiled down at Fredricka, ignoring Colin altogether. "But I think you ought to have a second chance with me. I'm not self-ish—I'm willing to share."

"I'm not." Colin pulled Fredricka close to him.

Fredricka thought Colin was just being gallant to claim her, but Colin's voice was again that strange, soft tone. Fredricka thought, here Colin had been bellowing all those years, and was ignored, and now he spoke softly and everybody's ears perked up. An interesting phenomenon.

Vinnie chided Colin in good humor, "Not only don't you share, but you're selfish."

"Yes."

Fredricka laughed and suggested, "Our Queen could handily endure some praise."

"That one's a sponge. It would take something like a prayer wheel to keep her from feeling neglected."

"Then go help out." Fredricka gestured.

Vinnie countered, "If I do this for the good of the community, and as a payment on my obligations as a guest, will you give me a dance tonight?"

Fredricka looked at Colin.

But Colin only stared stonily at Vinnie and gave no reply.

So Vinnie said to Fredricka, "I'll do my share, feeding the Queen's ego. And you arrange yours, saving me a dance. Okay?"

Fredricka replied, "I'm with Colin."

And Colin smiled.

But Vinnie laughed, undeterred, and went off in Sheila's direction.

Colin took Fredricka's elbow in one of his ham hands and guided her through the fisherpeople, the hot-dog eaters and the loiterers to his car. He put her inside and took her away from there to one of the isolated side roads. There he stopped the car, got out, opened the trunk and got out a blanket. He came around and encouraged a suddenly hesitantly eager Fredricka out of the car. He escorted her over by a stand of gnarled mesquite trees. He let go of her arm, stomped around quite thoroughly and then spread the blanket in the rather unkempt batch of black-eyed Susans. He sat down and held out a hand to her as he said "Come here and kiss me. You've tried my patience enough for one day, and you owe me two. I can handle two. Come here."

With remarkable self-restraint, she didn't rush over, knock him flat and attack him. She'd been waiting all day for a kiss; and there they were, out in the middle of nowhere with no possibility of interruption. Now she could find out which of them was the shockingly out-of-control sexual being.

She smiled at him.

In that quiet way he'd begun to perfect, he warned her, "If I have to come fetch you, it'll cost you extra."

She said, "Will you look at all the black-eyed Susans!" She glanced around with great interest and chattered, "Why, I haven't seen any in an age or two. Momma would love a bouquet. Is that why we stopped?'' She looked at him brightly. ''Has Momma told you she just loves wildflowers?''

''I gave you fair warning.'' And he came to his feet effortlessly.

She said, ''Uh-oh.'' And she backed away a little.

He saw clearly that she wasn't at all afraid of him. She was biting her lower lip so she wouldn't smile. She was *teasing* him!

He stalked her, moving carefully, following her, herding her. It was easy to do because she wasn't watching where she was going—she was watching his eyes.

When she stepped backward onto the blanket, she looked down in surprise, and he had her.

He tugged her down as she was saying ''How did I get here? Now wait a minute. Uhh...''

And he kissed her. He did a really thorough job of it. He held her across him, his arms were just right, his hard chest felt great to her body and his mouth was perfect on hers. The right greediness and savoring. The right coaxing. And his hands began to move slowly.

He lifted his head and looked into her eyes. She smiled a little and asked, ''How'd you learn to kiss like that?''

He demonstrated his skill again, then he told her hoarsely, ''Playing the oboe.''

Her lips mumbled, ''You blow into an oboe. Kisses are different.''

''Your mouth has to make love to an oboe to get it to sing, and that's what it taught me to do. My mouth makes love to yours.''

Limply hanging in his arms, she had to agree he'd learned that part perfectly. ''Do it again.''

But he put her aside and told her, "Sit up and look starchy, or I'll go crazy."

She complained, "You turn me to mush and then tell me to sit up, all by myself, and look stiff?"

"Do I turn you to mush?"

"It scares me that you're beginning to look good to me when I'm in love with Sling."

"You just think you are." He dismissed any idea of Sling.

"But I've loved him since I was in the third grade. How can I be here in the woods wanting another kiss from you if I love Sling?"

He couldn't breath, but he told her, "You're a stubborn, determined woman and an adventurer."

"I am?"

"Yes. And I'll let you have one more kiss. Then we'll have to skedaddle or—"

"Or?"

But with her mouth so nicely ready, he kissed her. Marvelously. She felt like a scarlet woman. She'd never begged or contrived a kiss from Sling. It had never occurred to her to do that with Sling. She'd accepted those he gave her as a part of their going together, and she'd enjoyed his kisses. Sling didn't set her wild so that she wiggled closer and strained and breathed harshly through her nose and clawed her fingers into his shoulders. It probably should embarrass her, but Colin didn't appear to mind at all, at all.

Again he took hold of her shoulders and peeled her away from him to set her aside in a limp lump. Then he rose, reached down and lifted her to her feet and held her steady until her body adjusted to the change in position. He released her, shook out the blanket and folded it as he walked stiffly over to his car to put it into the trunk. Then he said, "The keys are in the ignition, you drive on home. I believe I'll walk."

She objected, "How can you walk? I can barely stand! How do you think I could drive, for Pete's sake?"

"I'll take you home."

"I don't understand you. How can you possible drive a car? You've gotten me all steamed up so I can't—"

He agreed: "You've gotten me pretty steamed up, too."

"—think straight and then you quit! Isn't there a name for men like you who tease and then won't?"

Very carefully he asked, "Do you know what you're saying?"

A little testily she retorted, "I can't tell which end is up. How can I know what I'm saying?"

He began to smile and his eyelids came down about half way. A strange look came into his eyes and his head and body moved in a very smug way. Not posturing or strutting, but in a way that was almost a restrained swagger. There was a confidence to him that had never been there before.

She watched him, cooling a little. She knew that how she behaved in these next few seconds would determine whether the blanket stayed in the trunk of the car.

He instantly saw the cautioning in her, and his eyes again changed. The smile stayed, and he still moved in that different way, but his emotional balance was altered. His fingers on her elbow were only guiding as he took her to her side of the car. He opened the door, but then he took her into his arms and laughed as he hugged her closely, possessively.

She stiffened a little and didn't laugh back or encourage him. So he put her in the car, then walked around it to get in and drive her home. They didn't say anything all the way there, but he still had that smile. It was one of self-congratulation in some strange way. She wondered why he was congratulating himself. Nothing had happened.

At the Lambert house, Colin stopped the car and came around to help Fredricka. No one was in sight. Colin took her to the screen door and reminded her, "You still owe me a kiss."

"I only owed you two and you took seven."

He laughed. "It was just one, but that's because of the way you kiss. It just seemed like more. You're a kisser."

"I didn't do one thing. You're the one who's the sex maniac. It isn't me, after all, it's *you*! You need to control yourself." And she walked past him and on into the house.

He was amazed. In all their lives, it was the first time he'd ever heard Fredricka make any kind of protest or give any strident opinion! Why had she declared it was *he* who was the sex maniac, not she *after all*? Had she thought for a while that it was she who was responsible for their flaming, flaring-out-of-control reactions to each other?

He was so filled with exuberance that he had a little trouble getting back into the car and driving far enough so that she couldn't hear him going "Eeeeehhhhaaaaa!" *Several* heartfelt times. So he had her attention, and she not only liked his kisses, but after he'd kissed her, she'd thought she was a sex maniac! Even more important: it was a new feeling for her.

So she'd never felt that with Sling! It was proof that she didn't love Sling. She loved Colin Kilgallon.

How was he going to make her realize that?

Emotionally exhausted, Fredricka napped gratefully. She wakened to face the fact that the day was far from being over. Saturday night's dance loomed. In such a place, with such limited accommodations, one dance had to be very similar to any other.

The same set of people would go to that same rectangular building, which would have frustrated yet another or the same decorating committee. The same band would play, and the musicians would allow others to sit in for the area standard of ten dollars. The place would be chock-full of a renewed supply of balloons and flowers, and in the darkened Hall, it would be noisy and hard to see. What anyone wore would really not be that important.

So when Fredricka's sisters came to her room to watch her dress, she was tolerant—until she pulled that skin-colored dress over her head and settled it on her body. She gasped.

Tate said, "You're supposed to wear a nude bra."

"But it'll *look* like—"

And her sisters chorused variations of "Of course."

Fredricka was firm: "I can't wear it." And she took off the cream dress.

"No guts," Roberta told Hillary.

Hillary replied, "Never had any real sense of adventure."

Tate said, "It's a buckling under to challenge. Sheila will get him."

"Get who?" Fredricka head snapped around.

"Sling." Georgina supplied with some indignation.

"Oh." It was then that Fredricka realized she hadn't been thinking of Sling as in danger of being gotten by Sheila. Didn't she care if Sheila got Sling? How strange.

So Fredricka didn't hear any of the other discussion as she chose a shirtwaist dress from her closet and put it on. Who had she thought of when threatened with losing him to Sheila? Colin?

There were taps on Fredricka's door as husbands went past on their way downstairs. And gradually the sisters checked themselves out in Fredricka's mirror and drifted away. They left the bedroom door open for her to follow, as they went on out of the room.

Fredricka looked at herself in the soft blue material of the dress and knew that Colin would like it. She smiled at herself in a strange, secret way, then turned toward the door and went into the hall. She could hear the voices of all those who were gathered below. They'd always been a big family, but now they had just about doubled. There was laughter and ready conversation.

Fredricka walked to the top of the stairs—and she instantly saw Sheila was there, sparkling like a diamond in the midst of rocks. Lambert sisters were akin to rocks? And Fredricka was the least of those rocks. She never hesitated. She turned right around, went back to her room and put on the cream dress.

Seven

———

When Fredricka came down the stairs in that perfectly modest, scandalous cream dress, there was a quick silence, even a gasp. While Fredricka hoped the gasp was from Sheila, she was peeking little flicks of monitoring glances at Colin.

He just looked, and he appeared to Fredricka to be quite calm. He didn't change expression; he hadn't been the gasper, and he didn't blush. So the dress wasn't as shocking as she'd thought. He could handle it.

She then looked at her daddy, who was smiling just a little, as if he'd like to chuckle out loud. Catching her glance, her daddy shook his head a bit, as he'd done when she was six and had painted her entire body blue. She'd wanted to be different. That had been before Tate's Tarzan period.

Fredricka then checked her mother, who winked, and her sisters all smiled at her with some pride. She came down the rest of the stairs, and Colin must have moved, for he was there to take her hand just in time to foil Vinnie, who was reaching eagerly for her.

Colin not only took her hand, but he did a barely acceptable, social shoulder-block on Vinnie. Colin then growled something low in his throat that was ear-catching because it was so menacing and was just between the two men. After that, Colin turned his look to Fredricka, and she knew she was in trouble.

Her glance fled Colin's so she was privileged to see Sheila's ugly envy, and that strengthened Fredricka's resolve. If Sheila coveted that cream dress, it must be worthwhile making Colin so furious.

He couldn't very well bawl Fredricka out right there in front of her parents, so he didn't get to really vent his spleen until they were in his car. And she did hesitate to get into such a small space with a man that angry.

It took some courage. She felt a little heady surprise that she could toss her swirl of strawberry-blond hair, as she settled into her seat, with a sickeningly sweet and smiling "Thank you" to Colin. It was a red flag.

He stood there with one hand clenched on top of the car door and the other out of her sight on the car roof...and he breathed. He shifted a couple of times, and she wouldn't have been surprised if he'd hauled her out of the car and sent her upstairs to change, but he just went back to breathing again. She didn't say a word but looked straight ahead and pretended he was being normal.

She had noticed her momma and daddy hadn't left for the dance yet. So they knew she was potentially in a bind, and they waited to see if they would have to interfere.

Finally Colin closed her door with exceeding care and walked around the hood to his side of the car. He opened his door, settled his bulk into that small space with remarkable ease, and closed the door gently. He started the motor, and she watched with some élan.

Colin glanced up, and he saw it all. She was on the very *brink* of being her own woman.

He realized then that he would have to handle the situation, that dress, and her, without disturbing this defiant bid she was making for her independence. If she was squashed now, she might never try again. So whatever chaos that dress caused tonight, and however tough it might become, he had to preserve this fragile grasp Fredricka was making in her harebrained bid to be her own woman. He hoped there wouldn't be a brawl. Then he smiled. A good fight might help him.

Fredricka was moving her head as if she were testing new ways of doing it. She was very conscious of herself. And she felt devastating. Then it occurred to her that she hadn't noticed—or cared—what Sling had thought of her dress. And she smiled and looked sideways at Colin.

His independent tongue just went on and asked, "What are you doing, wearing that dress?"

He was jealous? She smiled a little and lifted her chin quite sassily. "Attracting Sling." The gauntlet was down.

With a raking, hot-eyed side glance, he growled at her, "You'll be attracting, all right." Then grudgingly he added, "I'll probably have to wrestle every damned male over fourteen. You'll have their eyes bugging, their pointed little teeth salivating, and their hairy knuckles dragging on the floor."

She laughed deliciously. He could hear the new confidence in her laugh. If she'd ever just noticed, men had been like that around her all her life. She hadn't seen anyone but Sling. Now she was belatedly tasting the headiness of an eighteen-year-old woman who knew she was attractive to men. Colin sighed with endurance; then he smiled. He could handle it. All that he had to do was keep this situation under firm control, let her have this little fling, and then nail her attention to *him*.

Since Colin was acquainted with most of the other men at the dance, he could control how far those men would go in trying to attract Fredricka, and he had Fredricka's brothers-in-law as amused codefenders. Therefore Fredricka's tasting the heady ego sugar of men openly competing for her never got entirely out of hand. Except for Vinnie.

Predictably, Vinnie gave Colin the most trouble. Colin finally really understood women's talking about octopus-handed men. Blocking Vinnie's reaching hands was like stomping cinders flying from a brushfire. Keeping Vinnie in control needed all Colin's attention. But Vinnie loved the challenge, and he coaxed a laughing Fredricka to go outside to have a little sip of something nice. Colin knew what Vinnie had in mind, and wasn't entirely polite about thwarting him.

Fredricka could flirt with no trouble at all. She not only had her daddy there, but a bulldog watchdog. She found it was delicious to flirt safely.

Colin thought she was outrageous, until he understood that she was doing it for him. With everything she did, she watched for his reaction. She was trying to make him jealous, to get his attention. She was a slow learner.

He wondered if she really thought it was just that dress that was drawing all those familiar moths suddenly to her flame? Didn't she realize it was her attitude? She *thought* she was attractive, and she was. She *expected* attention, so she had it. She'd had both all along. She was only now aware she was alluring.

Colin sighed. She would have to taste the triumph for another couple of days so that she could finally know it was she and not what she had on that was the cause of the attention to her. And he made his own discovery that all men finally learn: women are a lot of worthwhile trouble.

Sheila came over to Colin and gave him her full-wattage smile. "You're the only man here who hasn't danced with me. You must. It's part of the package that I insisted was my right when they asked me to be Queen."

Colin looked down into the glare of her personality and thought what a clever tongue she had, but there was just something about Sheila that grated on the nerves. He still hadn't found out what had happened the night before when Sling and Lizzabelle had had to move Sheila's things over to the Comstocks'. But despite his mother's strident training in manners, he just didn't want to have to put his hands on this woman. He smiled politely and said, "I'm promised."

Sheila looked around perkily to indicate she could find no potential partner for him; and Colin thought, in any other woman, the movements would be delightful. How strange the same movements by Sheila were so irritating. Then he felt sorry for her, so he said kindly, "I believe I've been abandoned," and he danced with her.

He became increasingly impatient. Sheila never tuned down. She was Ms. Personality every single minute. It was wearing. He wondered why Sheila was the way she was. Insecurity? She craved admiration to such a degree that it was strange. Perhaps it was a lack of inner confidence, and she needed attention to feel she was worthwhile? Like Fredricka. Only Fredricka had never sought attention. Not until tonight, with that damned dress.

He asked Sheila kindly, "What do they have in Oregon besides rain?"

She sparkled and laughed. "Greenery."

He grinned back as he considered that she was quick. She had to be intelligent to be that quick. That part wasn't fake. But he forgot the puzzle of Sheila as he looked over the dark, murky, crowded, balloon-filled Hall. And he saw that Sling was dancing with Fredricka.

Sling was telling Fredricka that she looked "nice" and he danced with her clutched against him in his normal shuffle. He said, "There's Quint over there dancing with Bill's Jennifer."

Fredricka asked, "Now, how can you dance with me and look over my shoulder at the crowd?" But even to her own ears, she recognized that she was teasing him and she wasn't jealous. Sling was just an old friend. After all these years, she had finally realized that.

But across the room, Colin saw them clutched to-gether, laughing, and jealousy dropped green poison into his gut.

By the time eleven o'clock allowed the free burst-ing of balloons, Colin was like a leashed tiger. He wanted out of that Hall, but he wanted Fredricka along with him. Vinnie was dancing with Fredricka by then. He'd already danced with her a couple of times, and Colin thought he was pushing.

So Colin stood in the jam at the edge of the dance floor, ignoring everyone around him, and waited for the band to finish the piece. Then he plowed through the crowd and took hold of Fredricka's arm as the next tune began.

Vinnie objected amid the sound of popping bal-loons. "Hey! This is my dance with her."

Colin leaned close to him and growled, "Hear them pops? Give me any trouble and I'll pop yours." He said it deliberately and low.

Vinnie laughed; his eyes sparkled and he didn't give an inch.

Fredricka pulled free of Vinnie's hands and asked Colin, "What did you say to make Vinnie laugh that particular way?"

Vinnie gave Colin a hilarious glance and replied for him, "He said he wished he could dance like I do."

Since that was patently contrived and Colin's face was the way it was—very hard—Fredricka asked, "What's going on?"

Again it was Vinnie who responded. "I think all fe-males should have a choice. And under these circum-stances, I would like to be in the running."

Colin knew that Sheila would have instantly known what Vinnie meant, but Fredricka asked, "Some contest? Running? Are you two in some bet? I know you're not racing horses. What's going on?''

Vinnie then looked at Colin and said, ''See? I want my chance.''

Colin moved Fredricka to the other side of his formidably strong body and replied, ''No.''

This time Vinnie didn't laugh. He looked thoughtful and considering as they left him standing there.

By then it was hard to walk through the balloon debris now on the floor, but they could all see better. It was still dark, but there wasn't the barricade of floating interference. So Colin and Fredricka saw Sling and Sheila leaving the hall.

Fredricka asked, ''Where're they going?''

He'd promised never to hedge or lie. ''Where we all used to go. Tim's Motel.''

''What do you mean 'all'?'' Fredricka puffed in indignation. ''I never did!''

''I know.''

After a pause, she inquired, ''Why don't they just go to his place?''

Over a timid feeling of exciting realization of what she'd just said, Colin managed to remind her: ''Mrs. Comstock would know the minute Sling's pickup drove into his own yard.''

Fredricka nodded, agreeing to that. ''Tim's?'' She bit her lower lip thoughtfully as she tilted up her chin and smiled a little. ''I hope the place is overrun with cockroaches.''

Colin had to grin, but he was electrically conscious of the fact that she'd said that airily and without rancor. She was cured of Sling? He told her, ''Let's go.''

''To Tim's? No, thanks.'' She gave Colin a really sassy, half-smiling look over her shoulder. ''The band's winding down. I think I'll drink half a beer and sing along."

"You don't need any beer to sing with the band. Just go ahead and do it."

Challenged, she gave him a confident smile, turned, walked over the balloon debris and through the thinning crowd to the bandstand. She sang the next number, "That Old-Time Rock and Roll," and the place came apart! Everybody still there got into the act. They all sang, the whole place appeared to writhe, and it was wild. All but Colin, who just watched Fredricka.

When it was over, she came back to him through all the shouts and laughter and whistling, and she was flushed and laughing, but she was looking only at Colin. He lifted her up and held her high, and those around shouted and applauded.

She looked down into Colin's face and said, "You're right. I didn't need the beer. I just needed everyone else a little loose and tolerant."

So she still didn't know her own strengths. But she was about as full of herself as she could be at that point, and she was sassy. He set her down and she turned away from him with a really flirting, half-smiling look back over her shoulder at him.

He said low in his throat, "You'd better be very careful, Fredricka Lambert, or I'm gonna get you."

She stepped back, leaned her shoulder against the side of his chest and tilted her head up the additional distance caused by her being closer to him. She inquired, "Oh? Who says?"

Colin focused across the room on her father, knowing that would steady him. Then he lectured himself vigorously about her needing a little more time as a flirt, to get it out of her system. But while his mind was doing that, his tongue said, "I have a couple of kisses coming to me, and I want them properly done, somewhere we won't be interrupted."

Since her eyelids were so heavy, Fredricka had to tilt her head up more, and that brought her mouth closer, so he almost kissed her. But he didn't, because she'd lifted it to him expecting to be kissed. He said, "The kisses you owe me can't be given in a crowded room."

She watched his mouth as she whispered very slowly, "Why not?"

And he knew he had a problem. How was he going to kiss her the way he wanted to kiss her, and yet not seduce her? Tonight was not the night to make love to Fredricka. She'd think it was the dress. Woman were a strain on a man.

They left the dance easily enough, and he took her out to that same deserted road, but they found a car already there. So he had to find another place. Then he kissed her until her eyes spun, and she lost count of how many kisses she was given.

He only just barely refrained from stripping off that modestly naked dress, but while his will did control his need, his hands confirmed that she was really very female. It was a real trial to let go of her and take her home.

She didn't object, because by then she was again mush.

He wasn't.

On Sunday morning Fredricka dressed carefully in an oatmeal-colored summer suit with a cherry-red blouse that peeked from the slit in the jacket. When Colin came to take her to church, Fredricka was

alerted to his look. She'd caught brief glimpses of it
before. It reminded her of something rather dangerous that she'd seen. What? Where? It was a look that
had impressed her, and where she'd seen it teased her
mind. That did distract her.

The church was a classic white clapboard with its
steeple pointing to heaven. The floor creaked, so no
one could sneak in and surprise God. And the pews
were unrelentingly hard. Skinny old Gidget Apple-
gate was the only one with enough nerve to bring along
a cushion.

The extended Lamberts more than filled the family
pews and the overflow was absorbed into other seats
with surrounding neighbors. It was Fredricka's first
public appearance with Colin Kilgallon. Friday or
Saturday didn't count. Sunday church did. Fredricka
was so conscious of Colin beside her, living and
breathing, that she didn't hear the sermon. She stood
when Colin did, and she took hold of the other half of
the hymnal when he shared it, and she sang by rote.
She was trying to figure out where she'd seen the look
on Colin's face.

It was his eyes, actually—a look in his eyes. She
needed another look into his eyes. She glanced up at
his face but his light-colored lashes covered them as he
read the words, and all that happened was that he quit
singing. She looked at him again, then figured he'd
lost his place, and she pointed to the words. He began
singing again.

She thought he had a good, strong voice. He'd always been a loudmouth. It was the first time Fredricka realized he could sing quite well. Of course, he
was a musician. But she'd known musicians with terrible singing voices. They could "hear" and feel the

notes, but their vocal chords weren't able to obey their need to express music; therefore they had to resort to instruments to "sing" their souls. Colin could do both.

After the service was over, in the crush of people who met only occasionally and generally only through church or community business, there were those who came to meet the Lambert in-laws and look them over. It hadn't occurred to Fredricka that Colin would be considered her "catch," and she was startled.

"Here with Pig?" One toothy old lady grinned up at them.

Fredricka replied, "His name is Colin."

But that only set the woman to laughing in such delight that she covered her mouth with her hand and looked around to share the fact that Fredricka Lambert had a vested interest in Pig Kilgallon.

Colin said to her, "You'll convert the whole territory to calling me Colin."

A little snippy, she replied, "You should have said something Friday night, if you intended to be called Pig all the rest of your life."

"I like having you call me Colin."

It took a while to get away from church, and then they had to go home and change. Nobody could eat barbecue in church clothes. After they had all changed, Fredricka waited for Colin to return, but the rest of the family walked out to a back pasture, which had long ago become the natural gathering place for the barbecue and the horse races.

It was a field that Jaff left fallow for that purpose. It had been mowed in the early winter, so the spring and summer wildflowers now ruled. The field was filled with black-eyed Susans, verbenas, Queen Anne's lace and mustard.

The barbecue committee had been in the back pasture in relays for three days getting the meat roasted just right over a slow, smokeless fire. It was so tender by the third day that it could be cut with a fork, and there was only the ghost of a wood taste. No sauce was used at all.

Long tables were set up for serving, and another committee was in charge of cleanup. Since the land belonged to the Lamberts, the family members were never on either of those committees because they tended to be bossy and try to run things.

Colin was a bit late coming to fetch Fredricka, and she was a little piqued. He was going to race a couple of his horses, and it seemed careless of him not to be there on time. She was impatient as she waited. Then she realized he probably wouldn't be too hungry for the barbecue, and the only reason she was impatient was that she wanted to see him. It wasn't really to "see" Colin. It was just that she wanted the opportunity to study that strange look in his eyes, if it was still there—what sort of look it was, and why it was there, that was all.

So everybody else had trailed off to the back pasture, and Fredricka was alone in the house when Colin's pickup came down the lane. She went out on the porch, but for some reason, she didn't go down the steps. She just stood there by the front door and waited.

He appeared to expect that, because he didn't hesitate. He got out of the truck and closed the door, then he came on up the steps toward her, not hurrying, but a little deliberate. And that look was still there.

The look scared her insides in a very exciting way. Where had she seen that before? It hadn't ever been in Sling's eyes.

In that low, quiet voice Colin used now, he said, "You owe me a kiss for church."

"Now, how can you involve God in a kiss?"

"God understands. I've discussed you with Him."

She was deliberately prolonging the time before he kissed her. She fully intended that he would. She smiled a little sassy and said, "I'll think about it."

"You want a ride to the barbecue? Then you got to keep the tab clear. You can't let debts mount up. You know that. That's what gets people bankrupt. Remember John Connally? He had to sell off the whole shebang."

Fredricka put her nose in the air and pretended to start off as she said, "I'll walk."

But he knew what to do, and he reached out a big hand, pulled her into his arms and against his body, and he kissed her again.

She didn't want to go to the races. She wanted to take Colin out and walk hand in hand among the mesquite trees and the cactus and lie under one of the oaks in the old leaves and the new grasses and listen to the mockingbirds. She wanted the breeze to play in her hair and she wanted to smile at Colin and tickle his nose with the new grain heads of the lush weeds. And she wanted to tease him . . . deliciously.

Colin hustled her down the steps and into the pickup and took her down to the pasture where everyone else was already eating. She knew Colin was smart because everyone noted they were close to the right time in getting there, that she and Colin had probably just been kissing but nothing more. People kept track of such things. Colin had been right to hurry them along.

Sling smiled at them, and Sheila came over and ignored Fredricka to ask if Colin was going to race. Colin said he was. Sheila took a ribbon from the back of her hair and started to tie it around *Colin*'s arm!

Fredricka was still drawing in a furiously indignant breath when Colin said, "I've got Fredricka's favor right here." He touched his left shirt pocket. Sheila handled Colin's rejection very nicely, and after a minute, she left them standing there as she went on about her Queenly duties.

"What favor?" Fredricka asked, still a little hostile.

"Your kiss. That's what you gave me to wish me luck in the races. I'll need it because you know Priss doesn't see any sense in racing. She's a remarkable quarter horse, but racing seems dumb to her. No sense of competition. But you need to remember that you still owe me for church and now the barbecue. With the races coming up, you'll owe me three by tonight when I take you to the cakewalk at the Hall. Then there's the fireworks."

Five kisses tonight. She'd get five. Her back prickled and she felt a marvelous lick of anticipation.

She didn't reply to his kiss tabulation. But she wasn't thinking about food as she ate the barbecued beef and the coleslaw, the German potato salad and the fruit salad, and one of Grandmaw Pritchard's hard rolls. Fredricka's momma had told her long ago that if for no other reason than being polite about it, each time she had to, she was to eat one of Grandmaw Pritchard's rolls, because the exercise was good for her teeth and gums.

Vinnie came over to say hello in order to taunt Colin with his presence near to Fredricka, and to confirm that Colin was going to race. Not too surprisingly, Vinnie was a stranger to horses and had no interest in a closer acquaintance with one. He volunteered to take care of Fredricka while Colin raced. Colin declined the offer. Fredricka smiled and introduced Vinnie to one of the Schultz daughters.

The races were for quarter horses, and the course was out to a hackberry tree, around it and back to the starting cedar stump. Wearing work saddles, two horses were raced at a time, ridden by the owners. There was no nonsense about weight trim or trying to get someone more skilled to ride. It was down to a man and his own horse.

The betting was quarrelsome and hilarious. And outrageous, since it was being done just after all those good citizens had been to church. Those women who didn't bet were disgusted and rolled their eyes at one another, but all the rest indulged.

Fredricka knew the caution "Now don't bet the rent" was kind of silly, since those Texas natives didn't rent anything or even buy on time. She knew some folks had been hard hit by the oil bust and the resulting tumbling of fortunes, but in that area, nobody had gone under. The steadiness came from old money that had seen hard times before then.

Colin's favorite horse Priss was an independent thing. Colin had shown Fredricka the very spot between Priss's ears that she liked having scratched. Colin knew Fredricka had to be a natural for scratching itchy places.

With the race in the offing, Colin had to go over and pet the horse and get her into a good humor in order for her to agree just to race. Winning was out of the question. He gave Priss a carrot but then, before the ride, he gave her a caramel with enough time for her tongue to fool with it until it was gone.

As with any race, there was a lot of shouting and shrieking and hullabaloo, and it was an exciting afternoon. Priss didn't win, but she did make a good showing. Colin knew that if she ever caught the fever of competition, she'd be a blazer.

Since there was no other challenge available, Jaff Lambert rode a cantankerous mule that had a natural violent aversion to being ridden. Jaff was pitched and fell, breaking his arm. Ethel fainted, and the daughters were more alarmed about their mother than their stupid father. He was lucky not to have broken his neck and they all scolded him. But his sons-in-law helped carry the pair to Colin's pickup and take them in to the hospital to be checked out and patched up.

Colin came back to Fredricka and took hold of her hands as he said earnestly, "I'll get Jim's car and take you to the hospital so you can be with them." That strange look wasn't in his eyes as he spoke, he was just serious.

Watching for it, still intrigued, Fredricka replied, "No. I want to stay and watch you race with Sling. Mother told us she was shamming it just to teach Daddy a lesson. Did you see how white he got when he saw her on the ground? She'd had to kick Roberta out of the way so he *could* see her, helpless on the ground that way. She was furious with him."

Colin shook his head just once. "She scared hell out of me. She's so fragile."

Fredricka snorted. "Baloney!"

"She isn't?"

"Momma is a preserver. She wants Daddy to cut out riding mean horses—or mules. She's decided to take a hard line on this. If he doesn't realize she's shamming, he can quit with honor—for her sake. Don't tell."

"Never." He looked at her for a minute. "Would you fool a man that way?"

"I didn't get any of the dramatic ability that runs in the family. Tate got more than her share, but she got my share, too. I'm just me." She looked up at him with simple innocence.

Thoughtful, Colin nodded once, very, very slowly, as he watched Fredricka. "They've borrowed my truck to take your parents into town. You owe me a kiss for that."

She didn't mention that she had four sisters who shared her parents, but she bravely took all the responsibility onto herself. "Well, darn. If I would have known, I might have found a free truck for them."

He nodded then, in tiny, tiny bobs of agreement. "That's why I didn't mention the price at the time."

That look had crept back into his eyes, and that strange, scary excitement shivered way down inside her body.

Colin was wondering if she wanted Sling's horse to beat Priss.

He went down and had a long conversation with Priss. He scratched her between her ears, where she *loved* it, and he sweet-talked her and told her she could so win if she just put her mind to it. It was important. And his whole life might depend on it. She put her head under his hand for more scratching, and he scratched and sweet-talked some more.

His sweet talk almost worked—the race was a tie. Sling grinned at Colin as their horses raced a little farther than was really necessary, and when they stepped down from their saddles, Sling said, "I held him back as well as I could without bringing him down on his rump."

Colin had kissed Priss's nose and scratched her where she itched. He scoffed at Sling's remark. "Did you see how Priss tried to keep him off her tail? She had to run alongside to make him *look* like he was a gentleman and not embarrass the ladies."

"Now you *know* he has no interest in mares. He considers her just one of the boys."

"Tell him that."

So Priss got a blue ribbon. It was Sheila who presented it to Colin, but he turned his head so that she missed his mouth and just kissed his cheek. Then he put the ribbon on Priss's bridle and kissed *her* cheek.

Since Colin was doing that, he didn't watch Fredricka as Sheila gave Sling his blue ribbon and kissed Sling's mouth. Sling accepted that nicely, kissing her back. Colin didn't look up until everyone laughed and clapped for them. When he shot a glance at Fredricka, she was turning away. He thought it was in anguish at seeing Sling being kissed by Sheila.

Eight

To see Fredricka turning away from the sight of Sling kissing Sheila just tore at Colin's heart. How could a man who might have Fredricka's love, kiss any other woman so that she witnessed him doing it? Even though the kiss had only been a "nothing" salute, seeing it had hurt Fredricka. Of course, such a kiss was the only kind that Colin had ever seen Sling give to Fredricka.

While most men didn't give greedy, passionate kisses to their loves in public, Sling hadn't ever appeared to...want...Fredricka. When a man had been away from a woman, there were indications that showed he was glad to see her. His eyes would be intent on her. His face would flush, his smile would be different, his hands would grip even just her shoulders. And his kiss wouldn't be cousinly.

Colin took off the saddles and rubbed his three horses down, as he began to think on how to solve Fredricka. He needed a plan. So far, all his energies had been bent on just seeing her, being near her, and having her around. Now he needed to figure a way for him to get her.

He tied the horses in a string and gave the lead to the middle Gomez son to take home and put in the pasture by the barn. "Don't go in the house, Peter, hear? No smoking in the barn. Got that? Stick around and behave yourself. If I catch you cheating on my rules, I'll have your hide. Is that clear?"

Peter grinned. He was twelve and a good kid, but fatherless. His mother had given Colin control over him four years ago. The relationship had worked well. Colin watched Peter leave, walking and leading the three horses. It was good exercise for the kid to walk, but Colin knew that once he was out of sight, Peter would mount Priss and ride the rest of the way.

The Lambert parents were back at home from the hospital, and Colin's pickup had been returned. Colin loaded the saddles into the back of the truck.

By then Colin was convinced Sling hadn't ever really loved Fredricka. If he had or could, the feeling would have blossomed by now. Sling hadn't minded when Fredricka had left the country to spend six years in Africa. Even though Sling had had a burden of family problems to be solved, if he'd loved her, he'd have found a way to nail her down and keep her around.

No man who really loved an eligible woman would fool around as long as Sling had, and risk losing her. Not a woman like Fredricka. So Sling could never have been involved in a romantic way; he'd just relaxed into being an available escort. That had allowed Fredricka

to assume the time would come when Sling would realize he loved her. And being the loyal woman she was,
she had waited for Sling.

Now how was Colin to interrupt her loyalty to Sling
long enough for her to realize that Sling really wasn't
interested? Colin needed to give her another view of
the situation, in which Colin would become visible to
her—not as Pig, her old friend, but as a man. His
kisses had helped, but she wasn't yet committed to
him.

The only thing that Colin could do would be to seduce her.

That was the only solution.

Although the idea of making love to her was far
from new, the idea of planning on doing it just about
ruined him right there. She kissed so hot that she *had*
to be interested in him at a fine basic level. In all the
years that Colin had watched Fredricka and Sling kiss,
he had never seen the spark of real passion. But she
had admitted that Colin's kisses had made her think
she was a sex maniac. She needed him.

After tasting Colin's kisses, a woman like Fredricka shouldn't have to settle for a nothing marriage
with Sling.

Thinking on the waste of the fine passion Fredricka had allowed him to glimpse, Colin decided he'd
do it. He would seduce Fredricka. And his conscience
twinged as he wondered if he was manipulating his
observations of their relationship in order to satisfy his
desire for her?

He did consider that for a while. But then he
marked the fact that since the third grade, Sling had
had almost a quarter of a century to decide. Any man
who took that long to make up his mind permanently

about Fredricka had had enough leeway for any conscience.

Actually, he was amazed that Sling was so...
cousinly toward Fredricka. While there was no ac-
counting for taste, Colin knew Sling was entirely male.
He'd known women. He wasn't shy with them. But he
appeared to be shy around Fredricka.

However, Colin wasn't about to call Sling's attention to the fact that Fredricka was a superior female
who was painfully desirable. If Sling hadn't noticed by
now, it was just too bad. All was fair in love and war.

Win or lose the woman, Colin would have the prize.
He would make love to her. Then she could decide
between a passionate man... or Sling.

Colin looked at his love over there across the mill-
ing, post-race crowd, and his heart was washed anew
with his longing for her. How many years had he
looked at her from a distance, his body wrenched with
this need for her, wanting just to have her where he
could look at her? Forever.

In all this time, since third grade, he'd found ways
to be near her. To him, in a crowd, no one else was
really there. When he was near Fredricka, the others
were only shadows who dimly spoke and laughed. He
sought her out in such a practiced way.

He looked down into her upturned face and through
years of discipline, refrained from kissing her. "Your
folks are back home. Would you like to go check on
them?"

"Please. Roberta says they're fine. Daddy's arm
was only cracked. Bad enough but not ghastly.
Momma said his head's been cracked since before she
knew him."

"If she was so opposed to his riding like that, why didn't she do something about it before now?"

"The way Momma looks at it, Daddy had no time for adventuring, they were married so young. So she looked on his riding mean horses as a substitute for running off as a child and going to sea. Daddy's that sort. Apparently there was another couple of contenders for Momma, and Daddy just couldn't take the risk that Momma might be snared away while he was gone, so he married her just about as soon as they were old enough.

"But now she's beginning to worry that he might kill himself. She says she's given enough tolerance to this foolishness, and it's time for him to quit. I think he's just as glad. He's loved scaring her and having her glad he was okay, or worried silly when he was hurt, but I do believe he's been ready to quit for these last few years and was just looking for the opportunity."

Colin intoned: "Your parents are strange."

That made Fredricka a little indignant. "I never said they weren't!"

He said profoundly, imparting new wisdom: "That's why you girls are all so weird."

That made her huffy. "We're just like everybody else."

But her conviction didn't sway him and he told her the ultimate: "I know about you painting yourself blue when you was six."

"I was gorgeous."

He scoffed, "Even un-blue, you've always been gorgeous."

She looked up at him as if he was very bright and she had to smile a little. She shook her head and said, "You're just hoping no one else had the rest of that pie. I did save you a piece. But you can't have it until supper."

"Now how did you know I'm particularly addicted to your pecan pie?"

"I've known that since you could first chew."

He thought that was an amazing thing for her to admit—that she was conscious of his likes. If she knew he liked pecan pie, how come she didn't know he liked her even better? He had all along. Was he that good an actor? Outside that first kiss, long ago by the gym that night, he'd had nothing solid to go on all these years. If he'd known she knew his tastes, he'd have had some additional encouragement. He said, "Let's go see your folks."

"What did you do with Priss?"

"She's on her way home with Peter Gomez."

Fredricka frowned. "What if someone took her from Peter? What could a kid that age do? He could be hurt. Priss is a jewel and she drops superior foals. How can you send her off that way with just a kid?"

"Because Peter knows how to slide off that horse slick as a whistle. Since he isn't supposed to be riding, he knows how to do that instantly, in case anyone spots him on her. We've discussed horse rustling, and I've told him to skedaddle if anyone threatening should come along. Priss can take care of herself. She can be real mean. And anyway, anyone who knows about Priss also knows she's mine. I'm responsible for what's mine and nobody's stupid enough to test me. And I would never allow any predator anyway near to anything that belongs to me."

He looked at her in a way that ought to make her know that if Fredricka was his, neither would he have agreed to escort any other woman, nor would he have turned Fredricka over to any predatory man: him.

Fredricka saw that look was back in his eyes. She said, "I don't know of anyone who would try to steal your horses, but there are foolish people in the world, and one never knows. I just wondered what Peter would do. He's just a kid."

"He'd skedaddle, just like he's been told. But so would Priss." Colin's voice changed. "She doesn't like strangers around her. She's a strong, independent female, and any stranger trying to lay a hand on her would be in for a big surprise. It takes a strong man to control her." Priss was just like Fredricka was beginning to be. But before Fredricka got too independent, Colin had to nail her down. He knew how to handle an independent, skittish female, and he wondered if Fredricka thought he was still talking about Priss.

Colin and Fredricka didn't need to take their leave of anyone, since the whole kit and caboodle would all be together that night at the fireworks. The committee had imported an Irish bagpipe group to play. There had been some push for a marimba band, so the pipes advocators had bargained to allow the marimba band for next year, promising there would be no dissenting votes.

The pair drove back to the Lambert house in Colin's pickup and got out to go up on the porch where the Lambert parents were holding court. That didn't surprise Colin, because with the barbecue in the back pasture, there was a steady stream of departees who stopped offhandedly to see how Jaff was doing and to inquire with concern about Ethel.

Colin saw that although Jaff was no piker when it came to drama, Ethel had to be the source of the dramatic talent that Fredricka claimed to have missed.

Ethel was pale and languishing on a cane lounger. Colin happened to know that in olden times, the lounger would have been called a vapors couch. Ethel's couch was draped with a light cover, which Fredricka had purchased from the villagers in Africa to bring home. The pattern on the sand-colored background was so subtle that a languishing lady wouldn't be overwhelmed by it.

Actually, Colin knew that it would take one hell of a bold and vibrant design to compete with Ethel.

Fredricka saw that her daddy paced because his arm hurt. He was a restless man anyway, and now his anxiety over his fragile wife made him even more agitated. He kept a careful eye on her. It was a good thing all those people came by, so Ethel wasn't forced by Jaff to lie upstairs in their room, with a vinegar cloth on her forehead. This way, she could be entertained.

Fredricka greeted her parents by saying, "Sit down, Daddy. Give your arm a rest."

He replied reasonably, "I'm not walking on my arm."

Fredricka retorted: "But obviously, you did try to do just that."

"That stupid mule—"

But Ethel interrupted, "'Stupid'? He wasn't trying to ride *you*."

Jaff was indignantly surprised that she hadn't known. "That mule did, too, try to ride me! How do you think I got on the bottom?"

As the rest came by on their way to their own homes, the porch gradually collected the Lambert daughters with their husbands, the husbands' guests and the two children, but the others only paused before they went on.

Then Sling and Queen Sheila came along and plopped down to stay.

There was tea and beer, and in an undertone only for Fredricka, Colin urged her to have a beer.

She scoffed, "You want me to sing? We both know I don't need beer to get up and sing."

"True. But since beer freed you for that first time, what else might you be tempted to try? With one beer, you're a wild woman, free and adventuresome. How about a half of one?"

She laughed at his attention. "No."

Colin watched her eyes sparkle and her face blush faintly with pleasure as he teased her. He couldn't remember Sling ever teasing her to make her look that way.

Through the years, Colin had watched. He'd learned that a man who liked a woman didn't leave her alone in public to entertain herself.

In all those lonely years, Colin had become an expert on how a man treated a woman in public. He sought her company, taking her things to eat or drink or asking her to bring him things or to look at something or to verify something. And he talked to her and teased her.

Colin had seen that a man did the teasing in a lot of ways. Sometimes if they were married it was only touching his thigh against hers. But with an unwed couple, it could be just holding her hand, or whispering nonsense to her to catch her attention.

Or it could be a man who coaxed his woman to drink half a beer because they had shared a time when she had, and her behavior had been a surprise to her.

Colin made Fredricka laugh in such a way that her family, and those people visiting heard. They then watched Sling, but he gave no indication that he even saw his woman flirting with another man.

For that's what it was: Colin's teasing was inviting Fredricka to flirt with him. She not only had responded to the invitation, she was enjoying it.

Next to her kisses, this was the biggest encouragement Colin had had. If she could flirt with him, her seduction would be easier.

It was then that Colin figured it out. After the fireworks that night, he would begin. It might take a couple of times before he could get past all her barriers and make love to her. Just the idea of making love to her filled him with a strange feeling that involved something beyond simply wanting her.

It was just lately that he had begun to carry protection for her, and he had been very sober when he had bought the supply in San Antonio. He couldn't make the purchase around home. He couldn't have anyone knowing that he anticipated making love with any woman. Such gossip would fly around the area like wildfire. And since he was Fredricka's escort that weekend, their busy minds would light on her. Along with teasing a woman, a man protected her reputation as well.

Would she marry him? She was a woman who committed herself full force. If he managed to coax her into making love, would she then feel she should belong to him? And he coped with the struggle of coercion versus fairness.

That was one hell of a struggle for a man who longed for a woman to the extent that Colin wanted Fredricka. But he wanted her love. Did she, could she, possibly really love Sling? Or was her attention to Sling only habit? Was Sling just a safe harbor in this world where men were scarce?

Could she come to love Colin Kilgallon?

He mentally groaned, there on that casually crowded Lambert front porch, among all those people. What did he have to recommend him to any woman, much less to Fredricka Lambert?

As they lazed around that hot May afternoon, the talk turned to swimming. For the sons-in-law, Jaff told how, long ago, the rock riverbed had been blasted for the pool. The water had been shallow until then, but that had been solved with dynamite. The site had been chosen because the fall of the land was just right.

Jaff told exactly how the explosives had been applied and how clever the people had been whose job it had been to dynamite it so precisely. They had blasted out a pool, rock-hammering and chiseling any rock lips that could cut the feet of swimmers. They had blocked the lower end with a wall of cement. There was a gate at the bottom of the dam so that the pool could be drained and cleaned. The cleaning had been done for that year. The pool was ready. But Jaff added, "Being springwater, it's just a tad cool yet."

The porch loungers were all so lethargic from too much food, social overkill and the drowsy day, that cool water sounded perfect.

An assortment of family and friends went inside to change for their swim, and Fredricka found herself in the remarkable position of lending Sheila a bathing suit. It was with a feeling of amazement that Fredricka allowed Sheila her choice, and predictably, Sheila took the red, sexy one. Actually, she snatched it.

But, as Fredricka thought philosophically, any bathing suit was very revealing, and which one she wore didn't really matter. She wore the blue. Then she dug out a couple of the oversize shirts from several years before, and offered one to Sheila, who smilingly declined. Fredricka warned, "You could freeze."

"I've been so hot for days, it would be a relief to cool off." She moved her forearm from the back of her head and allowed her body to move, wasting the pose on another woman.

Fredricka had fulfilled her obligations and said, "Suit yourself." Then courtesy forced her to add, "Wear your sneakers. You haven't forgotten the sticker burrs, have you?"

"Oh, yeah. We don't have those up in Oregon."

Fredricka could think of a whole lot of replies but bravely didn't mention any of them.

As they went downstairs in their suits, each of Fredricka's sisters found a way to touch her in congratulation for her adult behavior. Each touch was a salute. And her parents' looks to her showed they were proud of her. She laughed.

"What's funny?" Colin's low voice wanted to know.

"I've just loaned my best swimsuit to Sheila. My family is implying that I'm a noble creature."

He studied her a minute and asked softly, "And are you?"

"Not at all," she admitted. "That shade of red is terrible for her color of hair." After a pithy pause she added, "Enhanced color." Fredricka's eyes laughed into Colin's. She *knew* he would know she was sharing her bitchiness just with him.

Her sharing thrilled him. That she would reveal that earthy feeling to him was remarkable. No Lambert was *ever* caught being snide. It was a matter of honor. But she'd allowed him to see a part of her that she showed no one else.

He wanted to kiss her so badly that he could taste her. Amid all that gathering crowd of Lamberts and in-laws, he looked at her mouth as they stood in the lower hall of the Lambert house. And he felt as if he was alone with Fredricka.

Tate and Hillary passed by. The two pregnant sisters were going to nap. Benjamin decided he would, too, so he could be sure to stay awake that evening to watch the fireworks. Jenny and a Kilgallon cousin voted to swim for a while, then nap so they, too, could last through the evening's festivities. And Colin found he was a part of a group, tenuous as the others might be.

The swimmers walked toward the pool. The ground was dry and everyone had shoes on. Fredricka walked with Colin. The others milled and shifted, but Colin stayed beside Fredricka, and she accepted that he would.

He asked her with some interest, "Have you outgrown jumping into the pool, or do you ease into the cold water now? Have you changed?"

She gave one nod in formal agreement with her declaration, "I'm a leaper. And as I recall, you always ran ahead, leaped in, then got out immediately so that you could leap in again and splash cold water on everyone else. Do promise me you've changed."

He replied thoughtfully, "I don't believe so, but how can I tell?"

She turned to the others and shouted, "Watch out for Colin! He always splashes everyone, do you remember that?"

The rest shouted protests. So Fredricka put her arms around Colin with great bravery and yelled, "Run! I'll hold him until you all get wet. Hurry! He's bigger than I, and I can't hold him forever!"

Most of the rest fled, yelling. Vinnie said, "Then you can hold me. I'm a splasher, too."

Colin moved as if Fredricka were an ant. Vinnie left with great cries of terror that were terribly fake, and Colin became immobile again.

Fredricka rested her chin on Colin's chest and looked up at him. "You've been just pretending that I could hold you still."

"Honey, you can hold me dead-still anytime you want."

"Do you mean you would fake being helpless?"

In a very husky voice he said, "I'm completely helpless with you holding me. It's like Delilah cutting Samson's hair. You make me kitten-weak."

"That isn't true at all. And you promised never to lie to me. When Vinnie wanted me to hold him, you moved as if I didn't have a finger on you, and I was holding you with all my might."

"The outside threat to you charged my dead batteries."

The shout came: "We're all in, Fredricka. You can let him go."

She stepped back a pace and looked up, watching him with a slight smile.

He said softly, "Who is going to protect you from my splashes?"

"I'm going into the pool with you."

"Let's go!" He took her hand.

"Wait!" she cried. "I have to take off my shoes and my shirt."

He frowned at her shirt. "I'm not sure I can handle looking at you without that shirt on."

"Close your eyes."

He did.

She tore away from him, down the trail, discarding her shirt. She flipped off her shoes and jumped into the water, then they *all* splashed Colin as he ran up, and he jumped in, roaring, and ducked everybody—but Sheila.

As Colin stood in the deep water holding Fredricka up so that she didn't have to tread water, she had her hands on his shoulders and she scowled at him and asked, "How come you didn't duck Sheila?"

And he replied, "I didn't want to."

Fredricka groused, "You half drowned me, but you didn't touch Sheila."

"Your eyelashes are all spiked and you look like a water nymph."

"I'm a magic one and I'm going to turn you into a *frog*." She gave him a tight-lipped, nothing bump on his mouth.

He laughed in his throat and took her under the water to kiss her properly. Improperly.

They all played keepaway with somebody's shirt knotted in a mess. And Colin guarded Fredricka effortlessly. He not only guarded her from catching the trophy, but from Vinnie's hands. He was so clever that

Fredricka was never aware that Vinnie had tried quite belligerently to take her from Colin.

Underwater, Colin tugged teasingly on her suit bottom as she leaped for the trophy, and she indignantly tried to drown him. As she wrestled for the trophy, he released her breasts from the cups of her top and she was so scandalized that she tried to make him eat the soggy trophy mass. He prevented that handily, and his eyes laughed at her.

They all played so hard that they kept warm. Quint was the surprise. He was a formidable opponent, and he took Georgina under the water on more that one occasion, making her laugh.

But finally they began to ease from the pool, panting, tired, ready to rest, lying on towels spread on the weeds.

It was only then that Fredricka saw how little Colin wore. His briefs were black and rode low, only cupping him. There was a long expanse of hard body furred with golden hairs. He was very close to being naked. This affected Fredricka as nothing else had, ever, in all of her life, except for the kisses given to her by this same man.

Nine

———

Standing on the riverbank, pleasantly tired from the swim, Fredricka wasn't really aware of any of the others. She was, however, vividly aware of herself as a female and the fact that Colin was there, watching her with that look.

Without meaning to pose, she found she had put her hands behind her on the tail of the shirt and had pulled it down as she talked to Colin—about what, she had no idea. The movement and the tugging bowed her body, put her chin on her chest and tautened the shirt over her lifted cold peaked nipples. She frowned because Colin was examining his hands, which he held up between them, so his eyes were shadowed by his lashes. She wanted him to look at her.

He was. He just wondered if she was deliberately tempting him or if she was as unaware of herself as she'd always been. He was unsure.

But Vinnie was aware of her. Fredricka was a little startled to note that Vinnie was interested in how she was conducting herself. While she wanted to tempt Colin, she wasn't at all interested in tempting Vinnie. He wasn't interested in *her*—just in women. And he came over toward them with the easy slouch of a man who is willing to allow a woman to admire him.

She said to Colin hurriedly, "Let's leave. Vinnie's coming."

She really didn't need to ask twice. Colin was thrilled to be a part of an escape with Fredricka. That she wanted to run off with him was so mind-boggling to him that he was hard put not to scoop her up and run. He allowed her to lead, in order to see where she would go and what she intended.

The fleeing pair called their goodbyes as they took up their discarded clothing. She didn't even wait to go into the bushes and change clothes. Her earlier idea of lying under a big oak came back and directed her steps.

So he knew immediately that she wasn't heading toward the Lambert house. Where was she going? Out of sight from the pool, she stopped and they put on their sneakers. Then again he allowed her to lead. Under the covering shirt, she wore only the little bikini. Her strawberry-blond hair was coming undone and looked abandonedly eager for a man's hands to complete the chaos. His hands.

His breathing had picked up much more than was warranted by their mild exertions. They both knew every inch of that land. They'd played there all their lives. So he knew exactly where he was the whole time.

She laughed over her shoulder. "Are you lost yet?"

Think of that! She didn't remember all the times they'd played here? Had she been so blinded by being with Sling that she didn't remember all the times *he* had been along in the mob of her sisters and their friends? The thought discouraged him a little. Dampened his excitement a little. But he didn't lag behind. He was constantly about five feet behind her, his eyes on her, not caring where she led him.

She stopped at last under the ancient sheltering live oak whose great branches came down to the ground all around, leaving a private hideaway about fifty feet across. She'd counted the rough ridges around its trunk once and figured the tree was over three hundred years old.

She'd brought him to this secluded place. Had she ever been there with Sling?

She told him, "They'll never find us here. This is my own place. Not even my sisters know about this one. Maybe Tate does, because she's an explorer, but none of the others. You're the first person I've ever brought here. Isn't it perfect?"

She was. She'd never brought Sling here. Only him. He was just about overwhelmed.

"Are you cold? I'll turn my back if you'd like to put on your clothes."

He managed to say "No" as he dropped his clothes on the thick leaf-covered ground. He looked up into the branches at the ball moss that clung along some of the branches, at the hard little green leaves that lifted to the sun's rays. He looked at her. It was a perfect place. With some calculation he dropped down on the clothes and held out a hand to her.

Surprisingly she came to him, dropped her own clothes and sat on them, turning her head away. "Listen to the mockingbird."

Colin told her, "That's a redbird."

"Listen. It'll mimic our canaries next."

And it did, full throated and lovely. Then it did a cuckoo clock, and went on to the rest of its repertoire. Beautiful.

He wanted to know: "How did you know it was a mockingbird?"

"He lives near here, and I've heard him before."

"Then you come here often?"

She agreed, "When I'm home."

"I don't much like the idea of you out in the woods this way by yourself."

"There's no danger."

He reached out and laid her back across his hard thighs. "Who would hear you scream?"

She smiled. "You would. And you'd come and rescue me."

Colin looked at Fredricka lying across his thighs as his body curled above her, and he asked her, "Who's gonna save you from me?"

She had a tough time keeping her heavy eyelids from closing entirely over the thrill that coursed through her willing body. She smiled a little and whispered, "Help, help."

He loved it.

His chuckle made her think of fingers dancing, touching on places inside her. She became breathless, and in struggling to breathe, she found she felt a little faint. She'd never fainted in all her life, and she looked up into Colin's face wondering what he'd do if she passed out?

Would he scoop her up and run all the way to the house with her? Surely not. There was a spring not far away. She probably ought to tell him about it so he could soak his handkerchief in it to put on her forehead.

But he *might* ignore her fainting mind and just take advantage of her helpless body. She smiled again, but she knew her lips had to be pale and that she must look helpless. She wished she'd had more experience with men. Well, no, she didn't *really* wish that. She was glad she'd waited for Colin.

She knew she'd never really loved Sling. But all these years, had she been waiting for Colin?

That couldn't possibly be true. Why would she ignore Colin for Sling, if it had been Colin all along? And she realized that she'd simply not been ready for a commitment until now. She'd needed the time to prove herself to herself. So she'd used Sling as a smoke screen to distract herself from Colin.

Well, now, that was incredible. No. It was true. If she'd continued knowing that she loved Colin from the third grade, they'd be married with five kids by now, and she would never have realized she was an attractive, capable woman. She'd simply have thought of herself as Colin's wife.

Now she was ready to be just that, and still be herself. She was ready.

She moved a little, lying there across his thighs. She was exquisitely aware of her body and its nearness to his. He was right there, and she saw that his attention was riveted to her. His face was flushed, his breathing ragged, and his body was like steel. He acted as if he were pretty ready, too.

She lifted her hand and allowed her finger to brush along his cheekbone. "Your eyes look like a wolf's I saw once in a *National Geographic* TV show years ago. The wolf had raised its mouth from a caribou's throat and looked right into the camera."

She listened to her busy tongue in some surprise. So *that*'s what Colin's eyes had reminded her of when he looked at her. A wolf! A hungry one that had hunted and found its prey. And her tongue had known that all along and had just chosen now to communicate the fact—not to her, but out loud and to Colin. He knew she knew. She gave Colin a cautious look.

He smiled.

She thought, uh-oh, but then she saw the humor that *almost* obscured the wolf look. The look was still there, but it was overlaid with humor. He not only realized she knew he was a hunter who had found what he wanted, he was amused by the comparison.

She lay in his arms, against his hard thighs, and she was very still. He took his time. His breath was scorching her, and his body was burning. She ought to be a little cool in a wet suit, but his heat enveloped her and had probably dried her suit by now. Her body seemed to have swelled, and the bits of cloth that represented the top of her swimsuit were too tight. She couldn't breathe properly.

Just as she was about to get annoyed with him for being so still, she understood that he was allowing her control of him. It was up to her. If she sat up and moved away, he would allow it; but if she invited him to taste her, he was ready and would.

She licked her lips and brought her gaze up to his mouth. And she knew he was in an agony of suspense. He was suffering. She needed to get away from him and allow him to cool. She didn't want to be cruel to him. He probably had no protection with him. And he ought to have a say in what happened.

How does one ask a man if he would like to make love with her? If he was prepared for such an event? It would *be* an event. "Do you have any protection with you?"

His eyelashes dropped over his eyes but not before she saw the fires leap there. His voice was husky and he had a little trouble saying, "Yes."

"Really? Do you always carry protection? Who did you have it for? Why—"

"You have to know I've been after your body since I knew why there was the difference between male and female."

"How long have you been carrying it? Is it still good?"

"I gave up for a long time. I thought you thought you loved Sling."

She pretended shock. "How could you have been so foolish?"

He shook his head. "You did give every indication of it. Did you make love with him?"

"Would that change how you think about me?"

He was positive: "No."

"He never even put his hands on me the way you allow your big greedy paws to feel around."

He gave her a hooded look. "You don't like that?"

"Uhh ... Yes."

"How? Like that?"

She smiled.

"How about like that?"

Of its own, her body moved to allow him freer access.

He smiled, his wolf eyes glowing. "Like that, do you?"

"Mmm."

"How about this?" He moved his hand insidiously. When she only gasped and writhed, he demanded hoarsely, "Do you like that?"

"Ye-e-e-s-s-s-s." And the laugh in his throat was just as exciting to her. But then he kissed her. It was the ultimate of all kisses. How could it be so different? The mental debate was swamped by the sensual flood that engulfed her and blanked her mind almost entirely.

He made love to her with his hands and mouth. Her tiny swim top apparently disintegrated in his heat, because her bare chest was against his hairy one and the sensation was electrifyingly exciting, shooting off sparks and running fire all through her.

The kisses spread her toes and her lungs quit. She gasped and clutched at him, and he laughed again, hugging her close to him. Then he lay her back, and he explored her with his touch, with his mouth, and she was amazed at how different it was from just reading about loving. She'd read a how-to book, and the words were very poor. The reality was remarkable.

She had no idea exactly what to do, but whatever it was she should do, she wanted to help. Her hands scrambled around over him, trying to get him closer. Her body was restless and aching, and she was surprised when she realized the hungry, urgent noises were coming from her.

He was filmed with sweat, and he trembled with shivers of desire. Of need. His face was gaunt and his hands began to scrub along her. His mouth was as if he were starved and would die without her.

Then she touched him. The air burst from his lungs on a sound so primitive that she was enflamed by it. She felt a thrill of power, and she touched him more boldly.

But he'd reached his limit of restraint. He fumbled into the condom, then he lay her back and took her carefully, watching her face intently as he sank into her with hesitation, before he thrust deeply.

Her eyes widened and then she smiled up at him. He wasn't distracted, but continued to watch her as he carefully moved, trying for control. "Are you okay?"

With some surprise she said, "Yes!" And she laughed a little

"Hold on. I can't last long."

Rather drolly she retorted, "I have quite a good grip on you as it is." And she squeezed him.

He sucked in air and closed his eyes as he became as rigid as rock. He said very carefully, "Hold still. Don't move."

But she was no longer an obedient "Jane"; she was now the free Fredricka, and she repeated the pressure. She totally wrecked his tenuous control. And she witnessed his ride to completion in what must have been a remarkable experience, if his reaction was any indication.

He collapsed on top of her, his heart galloping away, trying to escape the confinements of his chest. His breathing finally became somewhat less ragged. She said, "Interesting."

With a Herculean effort, he managed to drag his forearms up to brace some of his weight off her; but he hung there, with his sweaty head down beside hers, not able to move another muscle.

"Does this mean that you're through for the day?"

He kissed her cheek in a chaste salute and mentioned defensively, "I did tell you to hold still."

"Well, at the time, I wasn't sure why I should be still, and I rather liked the feel of squeezing you."

"So did I."

"The thrill is gone?"

"For now."

She suggested, "Why don't you just lie back and let me satisfy my curiosity? I have sisters, and the female body has never particularly interested me, but males are another thing entirely. Let me look at you."

"Have I stumbled onto a voracious sex addict?"

"I'm not sure. But I'm not the one who has fizzled out."

He could hardly stand to laugh—it took too much energy. But he dragged himself from her very carefully, until he was clear; then he collapsed on his side and lay sprawled and helpless, his eyes closed.

He fascinated her. "What a change in you! Why, not even a minute ago, you were all over me, eager, panting, and look at you now. Sex takes a lot out of a person."

He managed to form the word: "Worthwhile."

"I should have brought along something to read."

He lifted a hand and it was as if it were done by remote control, as if he were a marionette. The hand came over seemingly independent of the attached, sprawled figure, and descended to her head, which it barely waggled. It was the only indication he'd heard what she'd said about needing something to read. The hand slid off her head, cupping the top of it, then lay quietly like the rest of him.

She sat up, her body restless and wanting. She looked at him and was filled with love of him. He was sound asleep! How amazing. To go from such hunger to such peace that he would sleep. Men were different.

She looked down his body at the length and breadth of him. What a beautiful creature he was. She sat there on their clothes, naked, and drew up her knees to clasp her hands around them. She sat there, cooling in the gentle breeze, and was aware of the place where they had taken their first serious step into committed love.

His sweat dried on her body as she listened to the birds. She looked around their bower and knew that all her life, she would remember this Eden. The sun's light made shadows with the oak leaves and the breeze made the shadows shift. There were no voices or human sounds. They could be alone in the world. She and . . . her man.

What would happen with them? He was a marvelous man. What if Sling had been interested in her? And with the thought, she knew that Sling had never been serious about her. Had he known that she loved Colin?

She really loved this man lying beside her, so vulnerably naked, his body sated from hers. She had given herself to him. And he had taken her.

She stretched, feeling her body alive and good. She looked down at herself, at her reddened breasts where his rough chest hair had rubbed, at her hands that had held him to her. And she was thankful that she had never been tempted before to just try sex, but had waited for this man.

She looked over to his face and saw that he watched her. He was lax and contented, and he smiled at her.

He said gently, ''You are a miracle.''

In spite of her thoughts, she was embarrassed, and she wasn't sure how to reply so she was a little flippant. "I? From what I've seen, all woman are just about alike. I'm no miracle."

He was sure: "You're the only woman alive in all this world."

"From what I've experienced, the attraction is very brief."

"Feeling left out? I believe I can take care of that."

He rolled to his feet and stretched, marvelously, and she watched him. She felt a renewal of the longing; the need stirred.

He looked down at her and his eyes were the wolf's. He hunkered down, sitting on his heels and he reached a hand over to lay it along the side of her head. "I'm going to make love to you for the rest of the afternoon."

The most incredible thrill licked up her insides. But she said primly, "I have to eat occasionally."

"Not today. Today we make love."

"Can you . . ." Her words faltered as she looked down, and she mumbled, "I guess you can."

He took her hand and pulled her to her feet as he stood up. Then he held her naked body to his own. Her flesh was still sensitized and her core became excited. He knew that, and took pleasure in coaxing her back to passion.

His kisses were leisurely and sweet, his hands coaxing and gentle as he loved her. He lifted her into his arms and carried her around in their paradise, then he set her aside while he arranged their clothing into a neater bed.

He tugged her down beside him, and his loving became sweeter, more passionate. It was she who became frantic and she who coaxed. And he made love to her, taking her gently, moving to thrill her, giving her release. But he didn't separate from her. He braced himself on his elbows, murmuring to her, telling her how much he loved making love to her. And then he began again.

She was amazed, and somewhat reticent, but he persisted and finally captured her passion again, and this time they rode the wild crest of ecstasy together.

Then, replete, they lay in their oak bower, side by side in the soft afternoon, holding hands and lazily talking, dozing, waking to stretch and smile and touch.

The sun was going down. It was time to leave that magic place. They dressed reluctantly. He watched her with pleasure. He told her, "You look like you spent the afternoon with a hungry man."

"I did."

He pushed up his bottom lip and told her, "You didn't satisfy me."

"Well, darn."

"You're going to have to try harder."

"You've got 'hard' down perfectly."

He admitted that. "Now you understand why you've failed and have to work on me."

"Is this what they mean by a woman's work never being done?"

"I suppose you thought it was scrubbing floors and cooking."

She agreed. "And all this time it was ... ?"

"Yep."

She inquired, "How come no one clarified that?"

"It's just another thing left for men to do. No one ever helps a man out of doing things for himself."

"What a sad story."

"There's a way to help a man out."

"I hesitate to inquire into that one, it being time to be home for supper. Are you going to have supper with us?"

"Thank you, but I got to see to my place. I've been gone all day, lying around with some wood nymph who debilitated me. Why don't you come home with me?"

She was hung up on one word. "You're 'debilitated'? I thought you said I hadn't helped you."

They left their bower and began to walk toward the Lambert house. He told her: "The help is very temporary. You have to put your mind to it."

That did surprise her. "My...mind?"

"Partly," he explained earnestly in order to be helpful to a neophyte. "You have to think how to help me." He held a branch aside for her.

She walked under it. "How come no one has to show you?"

He put his hands out openly as he said, "Uh... Somehow a man just seems to know there's a problem that women can help him with." He quickly amended: "A good and kind woman."

So of course she asked, "How many good and kind women have you found?"

Hastily he replied, "One. Just recently."

"No others?"

And Colin shook his head slowly once as he appeared to search his mind earnestly, then he said, "None that I recall."

"How did you know about Tim's?"

He smiled slightly. "Well, the guys do talk. I'm not the one who mentioned the cockroaches."

"I've seen how tacky it is on the outside. It isn't hard to imagine how it must be inside. I just wonder how Tim makes a living with such a rackety place."

Colin couldn't think of any reply at all.

At that point they were hailed by those coming up from the pool. "Where've you guys been?"

"Wandering." Colin replied easily.

The others joined the pair, who stood and waited, holding hands.

Tate said, "I'm willing to put good money on the premise that we have barbecued-beef sandwiches for supper. Any takers?"

No one spoke up but there were murmurs of agreement.

Fredricka volunteered, "That's really not a bet. We've had barbecued beef every supper after the picnic since I can remember."

Tate said, "I really didn't mean the bet. I was just trying to lead the conversation away from what you two have been doing all afternoon."

Fredricka looked indignant. Colin laughed, and the rest didn't say anything but they all grinned with closed mouths to keep from laughing. Vinnie was intensely interested and his eyes raked over Fredricka in such a way that Colin bristled.

Fredricka couldn't leave it alone. She had to say primly, "I showed Colin around."

And Roberta, the stickler, said "You showed *Colin* around a place he's known since he could walk?"

Fredricka elaborated: "Places he's never seen before."

And Vinnie said softly, "I'd like to see those places."

That made Colin stop walking and put his hand on Vinnie's chest.

It was very tense, then, because Vinnie was delighted, and Colin was very hostile. Fredricka took Colin's arm and said, "I'm sorry I can't go with you for supper. I've really had enough barbecue for one day, but I need to do something about my hair. Being in the sun all day—walking around—it's just like a haystack." An unfortunate choice of words, which made the group choke.

Colin stayed sober faced and replied, "I'll be back as soon as I see everything's okay. It's casual tonight, isn't it?" He stopped by her as the rest walked on, with Vinnie dragging his feet and looking back at them.

She looked up at Colin and nodded.

Colin smiled and ruffled her hair a little as he said very softly, "I think it's beautiful the way it is."

"Is it so obvious that we've been making love?"

"They're just guessing. They might think we've done some serious kissing, but they don't know anything else. Pay no attention. I love you, Fredricka. This was . . . I don't know the words. Thank you."

"I don't want you to go."

"If I should come into your house and go up to your room with you, it just might make your daddy become curious."

She could understand that. "Hurry back."

He leaned and kissed her mouth with some wonder. "I hate leaving you. I just want to look at you. To have you close by. I've got a hard case on you. It's probably fatal."

"I'll do my best to keep you alive," she promised.

"If you want to keep me alive, don't wear that naked dress again tonight."

"I won't."

He instructed: "Keep it. Don't throw it away or give it away. Giving it away could cause some other inno-cent guy a lot of grief. Just keep it, and I'll let you wear it for me sometimes."

"You're very—"

Her daddy called from the porch. "Hey, you two! Supper's just about on the table! Come along, now."

Fredricka called back, "I'll be right there." Then she turned back to Colin. "Bye."

He just stood there, looking at her.

She smiled and said, "I'll see you in a little while."

He nodded. "I feel as if I'm seventeen and that I've got no idea at all how to conduct myself. I feel real peculiar."

"Yes."

Her daddy hollered again.

She went up on tiptoe, and kissed Colin's mouth quickly, then ran off.

Colin watched her go out of sight through the front door, then he had to look around to orient himself, get into his truck and go home.

Ten

At supper, the only ones who didn't tease Fredricka were Sheila and Sling, who just ate. He didn't seem to notice anything, or even to hear the others teasing Fredricka. But Fredricka was very conscious that Sheila watched her too much. Why? And Vinnie. He watched her, too.

Then, after supper, as the expanded group was leaving the table, Vinnie took hold of Fredricka's arm and held her away from the others.

She frowned at him and tugged on her captured arm.

"You're being nice to Colin. How about me?"

"Let go."

"I can be very sweet to a woman who would be nice to me."

"I may break your instep."

He laughed as if she had said that to tease him.

But then her brother-in-law Quint came along and Vinnie's fingers let go of her. Quint just looked at Vinnie. Fredricka went off, and she heard Quint's voice rumble; but at the top of the stairs, when Fredricka looked back, she saw that Vinnie wasn't impressed with whatever Quint had said. She did wonder at Vinnie for *not* being impressed. Quint was formidable. Why wouldn't Vinnie buckle down to Quint's orders?

That night's gathering was to be at the Coopers' field. It was the land on which the Hall had been erected. It was used for the fireworks because the field was so rocky that nothing grew on it at all well, so there would be no fire hazard with the Homecoming's closing ceremonies.

Fredricka put on the killer dress that was a black-purple. She had to because she needed to wear all the sisters' loaned dresses. There really wasn't time to wear them all, but Fredricka had to try. She didn't want any of her sisters to feel she didn't appreciate the effort.

She surveyed herself in the mirror. After all, Colin hadn't said to dress ordinarily, in jeans and a shirt, he'd just said not to wear the naked cream-colored dress. Like that one, this dress was also modest, but it fit well. It wasn't risqué or flashy; it was just attention-getting. Some dresses could be that way—subtle and still be killers.

What was she doing in this dress? And she really "saw" herself. She knew she wasn't trying to entice Sling. She wondered why he had allowed her to trail along after him all those years when he really hadn't loved her. He'd probably thought he was being kind.

Was she stupid?

And Colin. What was she up to with him? Did she really love him? Or was it just that he was available now, when she'd had to finally give up on Sling, and she was determined to marry? Had she hoodwinked herself into believing that she loved Colin? Or was her female self somehow using him to take "revenge" on Sling?

What was happening?

She paced and reviewed her behavior. And she knew she must slow down and sort herself out before she involved Colin further in such a serious commitment. She had been headstrong and foolhardy.

Colin was waiting for her when Fredricka descended that Lambert staircase. He was the only one there, so he watched her with narrowed eyes. When she came to the bottom step, he growled at her, "Along with a couple of other things, you jar my eyeballs."

With the fingers of one hand to her chest, she exclaimed, "You don't like it?"

"An old quotation that I never really appreciated before this, has suddenly floated to the surface of my mind. It was about times trying men's souls. I believe I begin to see there are such times. This will be another night of tension."

"Why would this dress cause you tension?"

She was really puzzled, he could see that; she had no inkling. He had never before known that women could be so unknowing. She probably didn't even understand what she really looked like in that dress or what it did to men who had any juice in them at all. He sighed and set himself to cope.

They drove in his pickup out to the Coopers' vacant and bare field. The sun was setting and the air was sweet. The fire committee had built a large bonfire in the center, and people were strolling around, visiting. Off to one side was a table set with beer and soft drinks. Most of the people were already there.

To Colin, every other man who arrived at Coopers' field had come specifically to see what Fredricka would wear, and not one was disappointed. It was interesting to Colin. He knew Fredricka thought everyone was just in a jovial mood.

She was unchanged. Well, maybe a little aloof. She undoubtedly saw that at first some of the women were stiff with her, but she more than likely thought it was because she had sung that rowdy song with the band last night, and they were censuring her conduct.

Colin watched, and he saw that Fredricka wasn't conscious of the additional attention from the men. Now she wasn't inviting it, so she didn't expect it. But they watched her. They tried for her attention.

And they teased Colin. One clown even had the gall to say "I'm *almost* happy I'm not the one that's got to handle that one."

Another told Colin, "I'll trade that new bull of mine for a chance at her."

"You've had a clear field all these years," Colin reminded him.

Yet another commented, "I can't believe I never noticed her."

And Colin cautioned: "Your wife would object."

And yet another sighed as he watched Fredricka.

Colin said unkindly, "Your trouble is: you got the twenty-seven-year itch."

"Is that what it is?"

Colin nodded. "Go take a cold shower."

"You got no soul, P—Colin."

Colin bowed his head slightly to acknowledge the name correction. "She even got you to change? That woman could move mountains."

The watcher groaned, "Oh, to be a mountain. Or just a big man like you. She moving you around?" His eyes glinted with his wicked humor.

Colin cautioned, "Careful."

That teaser contrived fright. "Yes *sirree*, bob!" And he pretended to scuttle away.

Colin speculated on how many variations of that conversation would be presented as clever and new that night. He sighed. Fredricka was worth the bother. Where was Fredricka? Who would he have to pry away from her this time?

But she was talking with her daddy.

Colin strolled over to them and said to Jaff, "You an iron man? Out here with a new-broke arm?"

"Just a tingle. No problem." Then Jaff remarked, "I can see you'll have your hands full tonight."

Fredricka asked, "Are you with the fire-brigade?" The brigade consisted of those men who stood on the periphery to watch for sparks.

Colin replied soberly, "Another kind of fire."

She frowned.

Then Colin's searching memory supplied the fact that her coolness with him had begun back on the stairs. She had been different when she'd come down the stairs. What had happened? He took her aside and growled carefully, "You okay?"

"Of course."

But she wouldn't look at him. Alarm shivered through him. "Second thoughts?"

"We hardly know one another."

Such a ridiculous statement scared him spitless. "Now Fredricka, don't—"

"There's Pauline!" She started away, then turned back and said brightly, "I have a ride home. Don't worry about me." And she left him standing there.

Pauline? Fredricka has been ready to put Pauline on a spit not very long ago. Now she was escaping in order to see Pauline? Colin stared after his fleeing woman. She was in a panic. She was trying to get back to being as she was before—safe. He couldn't allow that. She was a lioness. How could he stop this retreat of hers? And Colin's mind scrambled furiously. Or did she . . . really love . . . Sling?

Sheila came along, then, and curled the tips of her fingers into the back pocket of *his* jeans as she leaned her breast against his arm while saying her intimate hello.

He had automatically taken a step away from her, and she released him as if the separation was her idea. Her smile never faltered. That caught his attention. He remembered to smile, and in apology for his rejection, he touched her shoulder. She glowed.

The action made Colin immediately think of Sling's kind conduct with Fredricka. That was exactly how he was reacting to Sheila. Impulsively Colin told Sheila, "I need your help." And he began to talk about Fredricka.

After only the briefest flicker of dismay, Sheila rallied. She finally smiled over Colin's conspiracy. And again Colin was struck by the basic woman. Not only was Sheila intelligent, but she was a fighter. There had to be a way to talk to her about herself. That could be the excuse for them to be together.

He said to her, "Hang on to the the thought that I believe you are an intelligent woman, that you are really beautiful, and, that you're a fighter. Hang on to that until you understand it, then let go of it for a minute and listen."

Then Colin began the re-education of Sheila. "Now, Sheila, you have to let down a little. You can terrify a man." The words "on" and "exhaust" and "balance" and the like, were sprinkled throughout his lecture, as they walked around among the people gathered on Coppers' field.

They stepped around folding chairs and blankets and their heads were close as the pipes skirled sounds away into the vast Texas evening. Colin was telling Sheila that while men were attracted to party girls like moths to flames, they didn't marry them.

Sheila was listening soberly to Colin's words. And Fredricka's shocked eyes followed them the entire way.

It was one thing to give up a man because a woman was uncertain; but it was another thing entirely for him to accept the spurning so readily and immediately find another woman. Rude. Fredricka sought out Sling.

He slouched his deceptively dangerous-seeming body against a table and was talking to a calm group of men. She thought: How typical. This time it was something about stomach worms in horses. She stood obediently there—as she used to—waiting for him to see her.

It was the attention of the other men who smiled at Fredricka, that brought Sling's awareness to her. But as before, he didn't quit talking: he just lazily put out his big hand and covered her near shoulder with it, leaving it there companionably while he finished his discussion.

It was like old times, pre-Colin.

And Fredricka knew that Sling's kindness was charming in a friendship; but it wasn't enough, now that she'd tasted Colin. She patted Sling's hand and left him to his discussion.

She wasn't aware of anything but Colin talking to Sheila. They were completely engrossed. But while Fredricka thought she was isolated in that crowd, all of her family was conscious of the whole drama. And so were one or two others in that closely knit, widely separated community.

And Fredricka almost drank a bottle of beer. But she decided she needed to do anything this important under her own steam and without artificial stimulants. She took off her shoes and prowled after Colin, keeping him in sight, as the pipes encouraged the area's coyotes to compete.

Fredricka understood that she was jealous of Sheila, but was it only because she was with Colin? Or was it still because Sheila had beat out Fredricka for Queen of their high-school class, all those years ago? Could something like that rankle all this time? Fredricka had to figure that out before she interfered again in Colin's life.

It was only then that she knew she'd never wanted to be Queen back then, or she would have made a better push for it. She had really expected to be burdened with it because Tate had been Queen of her class, and it seemed an automatic deal. First Tate, then Fredricka. She faced the fact that even then, she would have found the duties boring. She wasn't a butterfly.

Then what was it about Sheila that irritated her so much? Fredricka tried to understand and dissect the problem and finally decided that there were just people who annoyed other people, and that it wasn't the fault of either one. You couldn't win them all. One man's meat was another man's poison. There was a firm basis for all those sayings. That was why there *were* those sayings.

So, Fredricka thought, she was genuinely jealous now, but only because of Colin. She didn't want another woman attracting or trying for Colin. She wanted him for herself.

Why in the world had she taken so long to figure that out? And she decided it was because Colin had always been there. There had never before been the slightest threat of losing him. She'd subconsciously always known that when she was really ready to marry, Colin would be there. Incredible. Could that really be true?

Whatever truth there was in all her mental straining, the fact was that Fredricka knew she would tear Sheila's enhanced hair from her scalp if that was what it took to convince her to leave Colin alone. How primitive. Yes.

But Fredricka knew herself to be reasonably civilized, so she would be courteous about it—at first.

But still not wearing her shoes, which might have hampered her stance, Fredricka lifted her chin and stalked across to the closely communicating pair. She took hold of Sheila's upper arm and gave it a courteous jerk as she snarled in a ladylike way, "Get away from him *and leave him alone*! Do you hear me?"

That was not the conduct or the words her brain had rehearsed, and Fredricka was as startled as the pair she had confronted.

Colin's breath sucked in audibly. And Fredricka assumed she had shocked him. She blushed furiously, but she didn't give up. She gave Sheila's squeezed arm another shake. "Is that clear?"

Since the pipes had quit and the applause had died, Fredricka's words were very clear indeed. Heads turned to the little drama, and mouths opened in surprise and then smiled. The extended Lambert clan was riveted. "Jane" was disintegrating like a shell and falling away from a vibrant, alive Fredricka.

Fredricka then turned to face down the disapproving Colin, knowing that he could do any number of things that would be very awkward for a woman who had acted so boldly. She would cope. She lifted her eyes to his to find him looking at her with that wolf expression and a marvelous, proud smile. She told him coolly, "You belong to me."

Sheila said in a low voice, "Everybody's known that for years. Would you let go of my arm? I don't need your fingerprints on my precious flesh."

Fredricka looked down and discovered her fingers were biting into Sheila's arm. "Oh. I am sorry." She rubbed Sheila's arm to restore the circulation. "You see—" she began earnestly to Sheila.

But Sheila smiled and said, "I know." And she kissed Fredricka's cheek.

It was the perfect exit line and gesture. Sheila then turned and walked away, a winner of a kind.

Colin said, "I told her to get into public relations. She's a natural."

Fredricka frowned. "Public relations?"

"She's smart."

"She wasn't trying to steal you?" All that work and worry?

Logically, Colin explained the obvious. "I'm not stealable. I belong to you."

"But did you know that? All this time?"

"Not always, but just lately there's been a hint or two that you might realize it."

She puffed indignantly. "A *hint* or two?"

He nodded in polite interest. "When you seduced me out in the woods."

Irritated, she exclaimed, "You are maddening."

He grinned. "I'll keep you stimulated." Then he inquired with some interest, "Did you have a beer before you accosted us?"

"No!" she huffed.

"Wow. What a tiger. Let's get out of here. Where are your shoes?"

"I don't know," she replied stiffly.

"Come on, you wild woman. I need some assurance you belong to me."

Only then did she become conscious of where she was and what was going on around them.

The coyotes were taking their turn, stimulated by the challenge of the pipes, showing how howling should be done. The center fire had died down. The fire committee was pouring water over the coals to smother them entirely so the fireworks wouldn't have any competition. The total dark revealed the billions and billions of Texas stars that other states and foreign countries never saw.

"I can't see." Fredricka stumbled after Colin, pulled along by his big hand.

"In just a minute."

"Ouch." She'd stepped wrong on a rock and hopped a couple of steps.

"Here." He picked her up and carried her. "You ought to eat your carrots."

Fredricka thought with impatience, here he was, carrying her off into the darkness to have her alone, and what did he say? He said she ought to eat carrots. Hadn't he ever read *anything*? He was supposed to say impassioned things to her. Instead, she was a little nervous. She said, "This is the most unsubtle sneak-away I've ever heard of."

"You didn't hear about this one. You're doing it."

"Everyone in the whole of Coopers' field will know we left before the fireworks ever started."

"Well, that's okay. They won't be surprised when they hear about us, will they?"

By then, he had managed to find the particular looming shadow that was his pickup. How had he known which shadow belonged to him? While she thought that, he took his supporting arm from under her knees and allowed her stockinged feet to lower *almost* to the ground—but not quite.

So she hung from his other arm, which was clamped around her back. She was intimately against him. His other arm came around her body to help the first one hold her. That hand spread out below the small of her back as he pressed her tightly against his heat. Then he kissed her.

As if on cue, the fireworks began. All the explosions and rumblings and burstings were a logical accompaniment to Colin's remarkable kiss.

Her senses spinning, her body reacting wildly, she needed him to say words, but his kiss went on and on and deliciously on.

Just before she went entirely mad, she realized that talking wasn't at all necessary. He let go of her and put her inside his pickup. He shoved her over farther and got in after her. But he started the motor, and they eased away from the rest of the vehicles and when they were clear he turned on the headlights.

She inquired, "Who do you think you're fooling?"

Surprised, he responded with "I didn't want the headlights to detract from the fireworks. Do you realize what all that costs?"

A little offended, she questioned, "You aren't trying to sneak away?"

"Around here? Not likely."

It seemed to take a long time for him to find the right place to stop. She finally asked, "Where are you taking me?"

"Somewhere private."

"Well, we've passed through quite a lot of very private countryside. There's no one anywhere around."

He chuckled in his throat. "Getting eager for me?"

"I simply asked where are you going."

"You have to know, sugar, that when those fireworks are over this whole entire place will be crawling with folks going home."

"So? Where are we going?"

"To my place."

"I can't do that. It would be scandalous."

He pondered over the fact that there was no scandal in making love under an oak or in his pickup, but she couldn't go to his place. "Then we'll go down the next gully."

"Uhhh . . ."

"Some problem?"

"I think we ought to go back to the fireworks."

"We're going to make our own."

He said that, but it seemed to her that all that they were doing was riding along the rough back roads.

He turned in at a meadow where there were no fences, crossed it and pulled to a stop under the shadows of the trees. They were concealed from the road. He reached over and dragged her across the intervening space and kissed all the resistance out of her. He was superior in doing that. She was as limp as a rag and her hands were clawing at his shoulders. He grinned down at her.

She eyed him as he pushed the double seat back and busily stripped off his shirt, knocked off his shoes and skimmed out of his trousers. It was astounding that such a large man could maneuver in so tight a space. Then he turned to her.

She was awkward and breathless, and he was busily figuring out how to get her out of her clothes. As he peeled off her shredded panty hose, he asked with interest, "Where'd you leave your shoes?"

"Back somewhere on Coopers' field."

"You left them there? Why'd you take them off?"

"I had to be sure I had a firm stance in case Sheila objected to my taking you away from her."

Colin was astounded. "You'd planned to...fight for me?"

"Whatever it took. I had to be sure I could swing properly in order to clobber her one right on her gleaming white teeth."

"Sheila has white teeth?"

"Probably. Everything else about her gleams."

"And you decided to tackle her? Cold sober?" he teased gently. "Without even a half a beer?"

"One does as one must. I couldn't let you get away again," she told him honestly.

Very gently he said, "I've never been gone. You just couldn't see me."

He kissed her with all his restraint gone. And she responded in kind. He opened her door with his foot, slid his body under hers and then managed to turn them so that she was against the back of the seat. He smiled—she was so trapped. It was so damned awkward. It was so good.

She loved it. She murmured sounds to him, her mouth eager, her hands dragging at him. And he had to break away in order to find the packets in the glove compartment and make his hands steady enough to function as he protected her.

Then he made love to her, moving deliciously, filling her as she wanted it. Stroking her. Holding back until she was ready, he took her up the spiral along with him, leading her, then hurrying after her passionate response, and flinging them into the ecstatic void.

Her feet got cold hanging out the door that way, and she bent her knees to put her cold feet on the backs of his hot legs. Her movement settled him lower into her and he sighed in contentment. She put one hand up along his jaw and said, "I love you, Colin Kilgallon."

"Me, too."

That wasn't the greatest or best-done commitment she'd ever heard about, but it did just fine. She allowed her fingers to play in his hair as she thought about him—about all the times he had come to see her—and she said, "I'll never forget when you came to Africa. To go out of that scared village and then to find it was you in that plane."

He murmured contentedly, "You grabbed me."

"It was just so glad to see you. It was so amazing to have someone there like me. And you brought all that candy and made the whole village sick with the chocolate."

"I was trying to help you with good PR. I gave you credit."

"You almost got us run out of there. You're just lucky the elder from the next village happened to come in. If he hadn't been an Oxford man, God knows what would have happened to us."

"Nothing. They loved you."

"They are so talented." She allowed her fingers to caress his hair in contentment. Then she said softly, "That night after Sling told me he was going to escort Sheila during Homecoming, and we were all on the back porch, how did you know to hold me that way and speak to me so chidingly sweet? Telling me to use only one side of your handkerchief?"

"I have nieces who get very upset with the world now and then."

"You were brilliant."

"I would dry all your tears, but the way I see it, is you'll be so happy with my loving, you'll never cry again."

"Why do you suppose I loved Sling so long?"

"You loved me before you loved Sling."

"You fascinated me. The pig... You just loved that pig."

"I honest to God thought I'd have to start lugging around another pig just recently. It was worth the try."

"If you loved a pig—and me—I'd wonder a little about me." She paused, then said in the amazement of facts that led up to something spectacular, "How amazing that Sheila came along to this Homecoming. If I'd been with Sling this whole time, I would never have . . . seen you."

"I sent for her."

"Brilliant."

Modestly, he agreed. "I know."

"I love Sheila."

"Let's not go overboard. I just had to save you from Sling. He's so weather-beaten and solitary that when he's old he'll be shriveled up like old leather, tough and hard. And I'll still be sweet and juicy."

"And all your freckles will meld together and you'll be a gorgeous bronze, just like God intended. I suppose all our children will be redheads."

"I haven't asked you to marry me."

Smugly she sassed, "Not yet."

"What makes you think I'm not just dallying with you?"

"Because you're scared of daddy. He has a broken arm now, but he'd get around to thrashing you if you just trifled with his daughter. And don't forget our new collection of kinsmen. They should make you shiver."

"They all told me they were on my side."

"To trap me."

"Your daddy loves me. I'll move in. You daddy's never had a son, and your sisters all married foreigners. Jaff needs a good Texas man in his house to back him. He's been trying to get me to move into the Lambert house for as long as I can remember."

"That's because you never knew when to go home! You just stayed and stayed and stayed."

"I was always hoping you'd ask me up to your room."

"Why would I do that?"

He sighed, long-suffering. "Back to basics again. You're a slow learner. Do you know that simple fact?" He lifted from her with care. Then he puttered behind the seat back. "I have a surprise for you." And he took out a saxophone.

She laughed in such a helpless way. But he licked the reed and settled down and played a moody, marvelously sexy piece. Then he put the sax aside, but the piece went on! He'd taped it. It was playing on the boom box just behind their seat, and he made love to her to his music. It was everything she'd ever dreamed—with the man she truly wanted.

*   *   *   *   *

Author's Note

Although Fredricka's story is the last of the Lambert sisters series, I find I'm curious about several men who appear in the five books. One is Jim from *Odd Man Out*. Another is Sling, who is woven throughout several of the books. Then there is Dominic—and Fiona—from *Goldilocks and the Behr*. And— But those are other stories.

SILHOUETTE *Desire*

COMING NEXT MONTH

#535 WILDERNESS CHILD—Ann Major
December's *Man of the Month*, Tad Jackson, wasn't about to be
burned twice by the woman who'd betrayed him—but the fire
between him and Jessica Bancroft Kent raged out of control.

#536 THE DIAMOND'S SPARKLE—Celeste Hamilton
Public relations man Nathan Hollister lived his life the same way
he drove his car...fast. Beautiful Liz Patterson could be the one
obstacle that slowed him down!

#537 HALFWAY TO HEAVEN—Katherine Granger
Lindsey Andrews wanted it all—the perfect career *and* the perfect
man. Jed Wentworth offered her both, but she couldn't mix
business with pleasure—could she?

#538 BEDSIDE MANNER—Jo Ann Algermissen
Though her job was at stake, Dr. Kristie Fairbanks was tempted
to give in to Joshua Hayden, the one man who could threaten her
career...and her heart.

#539 READ BETWEEN THE LINES—Erica Spindler
Sociology professor Katherine Reed needed a roommate for a
research experiment, and her old "friend" Michael Tardo kindly
volunteered. Unfortunately, he was still charming...and she was
still in love.

#540 CHRISTMAS STRANGER—Joan Hohl
It was a cold, snowy night when Virginia Greyson met Matthew
Hawk. He was the gift of a lifetime. But would fate take him as it
had so mysteriously brought him?

AVAILABLE NOW:

#529 SHILOH'S PROMISE
BJ James

#530 INTERLUDE
Donna Carlisle

#531 ULTERIOR MOTIVES
Laura Leone

#532 BLUE CHIP BRIDE
Audra Adams

#533 SEEING IS BELIEVING
Janet Bieber

#534 TAGGED
Lass Small

SILHOUETTE DESIRE™
presents
AUNT EUGENIA'S TREASURES
by CELESTE HAMILTON

Liz, Cassandra and Maggie are the honored recipients of Aunt Eugenia's heirloom jewels...but Eugenia knows the real prizes are the young women themselves. Every other month from December to April in Silhouette Desire, read about Aunt Eugenia's quest to find them worthy men and a treasure more valuable than diamonds, rubies or pearls—lasting love.

Coming in December: THE DIAMOND'S SPARKLE
Altruistic attorney Liz Patterson balks at Aunt Eugenia's attempt at matchmaking. Clearly, a shrewd PR man isn't her type. Nathan Hollister, after all, likes fast cars and fast times, but, as he tells Liz, love is something he's willing to take *very* slowly.

In February: RUBY FIRE
Passionate Cassandra Martin has always been driven by impulse. After traveling from city to city, seeking new opportunities, Cassandra returns home...ready to re-kindle the flame of young love with the man she never forgot, Daniel O'Grady.

In April: THE HIDDEN PEARL
Maggie O'Grady loved and lost early in life. Since then caution has been her guide. But when brazen Jonah Pendleton moves into the apartment next door, gentle Maggie comes out of her shell and glows in the precious warmth of love.

Aunt Eugenia's Treasures
Each book shines on its own, but together they're priceless

SD-AET-1

FOUR UNIQUE SERIES
FOR EVERY WOMAN YOU ARE...

Silhouette Romance

Love, at its most tender, provocative,
emotional...in stories that will make you laugh and
cry while bringing you the magic of falling in love.

6 titles per month

Silhouette Special Edition

Sophisticated, substantial and packed with
emotion, these powerful novels of life and love will
capture your imagination and steal your heart.

6 titles per month

Silhouette Desire

Open the door to romance and passion. Humorous,
emotional, compelling—yet always a believable
and sensuous story—Silhouette Desire never
fails to deliver on the promise of love.

6 titles per month

Silhouette Intimate Moments

Enter a world of excitement, of romance
heightened by suspense, adventure and the
passions every woman dreams of. Let us
sweep you away.

4 titles per month

SILG-1R

Wonderful, luxurious gifts can be yours with proofs-of-purchase from any specially marked "Indulge A Little" Harlequin or Silhouette book with the Offer Certificate properly completed, plus a check or money order (do not send cash) to cover postage and handling payable to Harlequin/Silhouette "Indulge A Little, Give A Lot" Offer. We will send you the specified gift.

Mail-in-Offer

Item	**OFFER CERTIFICATE**			
	A. Collector's Doll	B. Soaps in a Basket	C. Potpourri Sachet	D Scented Hangers
# of Proofs-of -Purchase	18	12	6	4
Postage & Handling	$3.25	$2.75	$2.25	$2.00
Check One				

Name _____

Address _____ Apt # _____

City _____ State _____ Zip _____

ONE PROOF OF PURCHASE

To collect your free gift by mail you must include the necessary number of proofs-of-purchase plus postage and handling with offer certificate.

SD-2

Harlequin®/Silhouette®

Mail this certificate, designated number of proofs-of-purchase and check or money order for postage and handling to:

INDULGE A LITTLE
P.O. Box 9055
Buffalo, N.Y. 14269-9055